John Harris Knowles

A Flight in Spring

in the car Lucania from New York to the Pacific coast and back, during April and

May, 1898

John Harris Knowles

A Flight in Spring
in the car Lucania from New York to the Pacific coast and back, during April and May, 1898

ISBN/EAN: 9783337381066

Printed in Europe, USA, Canada, Australia, Japan

Cover: Foto ©Andreas Hilbeck / pixelio.de

More available books at **www.hansebooks.com**

A FLIGHT IN SPRING

IN THE CAR LUCANIA FROM NEW YORK
TO THE PACIFIC COAST AND BACK
DURING APRIL AND MAY, 1898, AS TOLD
BY THE REV. J. HARRIS KNOWLES

NEW YORK
1898

Dedication

TO THE LUCANIANS:

"THE KING AND THE QUEEN"

"THE APOSTLE AND THE ANGEL"

"THE FAIRY PRINCESS"

"JUNO AND PSYCHE"

"THE GYPSY QUEEN"

"THE PRINCESS"

"MINERVA AND JUPITER"

"MERCURY," AND

"THE SPANISH COUNT"

THESE RANDOM JOTTINGS OF OUR HAPPY

"FLIGHT IN SPRING," ARE AFFECTIONATELY DEDICATED

BY THEIR FRIEND

"THE POPE"

CONTENTS

v

VIII

IX

X

XI

XII

XIII

XIV

XV

XVI

CONTENTS

XVII

XXII

XXIII

XXIV

A FLIGHT IN SPRING

I

IT seemed like a dream to be invited to join
a party on a private Pullman car for an extended
tour of close on eight thousand miles, all in
these our United States! Yet such was the
opportunity which was generously offered us in
this springtime of 1898.

It was to be "A Flight in Spring" of most intense interest. The journey was to embrace in its
continued circuit, from New York back to New
York, points as widely separated as New Orleans
and San Francisco. It was to traverse many
States and Territories, and was to be accomplished
with every adjunct of unstinted comfort and
refinement.

The expected morning when we were to start on our journey came at last, with that subdued wonder in it that the dream, so unlooked for, was really to be a fact. Bags and satchels were all packed, and with that happy feeling which always comes to the tourist when, all ready, he is safely ensconced in his cab, we sped to the Twenty-third Street ferry for the Pennsylvania depot in Jersey City.

Never did the great Hudson River look so beautiful or New York so magnificent in our eyes as on that early morning of April 13th, when, through and beyond it all, we could see in imagination the great journey before us, all made more radiant by a munificent hospitality which had made it for us a fact—"A Flight in Spring"—which we had often thought of, but never hoped to see.

To start off on such a journey, with a six weeks' vacation in view, even if undertaken all alone and in most prosaic economy, would be an event; but when one was met by pleasant friends and ushered into an independent, self-contained flying home on wheels, it was indeed something ideal.

Our car, the "Lucania," was a happy combination of well-devised space and comfortable arrangement. Let us recount its good points. We may as well begin with the foundation of all well-regulated homes, the kitchen. What a *multum in parvo* that sacred spot was! It held quite a substantial cooking range; it had lockers and cupboards, and glistening cooking utensils of most approved fashion. Already our *chef* was at his work, affording, in his own person, with all its good-natured plumpness, a hint of the good things he could evolve from the interesting scene of his labors. He was the best possible specimen of a negro cook, handsome, fat, and jolly. He filled almost completely his little kitchen; his plump and shining cheeks looking like the very best and most exquisitely finished Parisian bronze. Set off by the background of his cooking utensils and other objects of his serious and responsible calling, he presented a picture worthy of a painter. I felt, as I looked at him, that he was a genius in his way. His subsequent work did not belie my instant instinct of his powers; for, on a day long to be remembered, as we were speeding across one of the most arid spots of our journey, somewhere in Arizona, he served up a dinner worthy of a poet; then I felt proud of him. That day the outer air was stifling. Our car was speeding through vast stretches of yellow, heated sand; the sun poured down in full force; every window was closed to keep out, as far as possible, the all-pervading dust. A weary gloom spread over the liveliest of our company, and even dinner was dreaded, as the time approached for that necessary function. At last the meal was announced, and we all reached the dining-room in a weary, limp condition, when a surprise awaited us. The artist of the galley, our negro cook, got in his poetic work. I felt his fine touch at once when I saw that there was to be no soup that day. Instead, we had some delicate fish, served with most refreshing cucumbers on ice, the sparkle of which, in the dim shaded light of our room, looked like dewdrops. Every course thereafter had a suggestion of coolness about it, gently hinting at our languor and its needs, so tenderly known and intelligently relieved. Slices of fresh fruit and iced coffee ended a repast, with the thermometer at well over 100 degrees, and yet every guest at ease and at rest. I voted from my grateful inwards that, if I could afford it, I would gladly give our good cook a bronze replica of his own bronze face, as a humble token of my appreciation of his noble art.

Among the further perfections of our land yacht were separate and secluded apartments for our married friends and other privileged parties, and ample berths for less favored mortals; there was also a spacious dining-room, and a generous lounging place at the end of the car, where after-dinner chats could be indulged in and mornings happily passed while watching the landscape as it seemed to fly past us and vanish in the ever-changing distance. But let us return to the events of our first day's trip. The marshes of the Hackensack valley were soon crossed, and at our first stop, at Newark, we rejoiced to find the Rev. Dr. Frank Landon Humphreys and his sweet wife, who were to make us glad with their company as far as Washington; and certainly this was done. There were quips and jokes without number from the ever versatile Doctor; and roars of good-natured fun, which he provoked, made us oblivious of the naked landscape, as yet with little more than a hint here and there of the coming springtime.

We had summer along with us, however, if good nature and pleasant chat can symbolize the warmth and comfort of that happy season. The ladies' bonnets and wraps, discovered by the Reverend Doctor in one of the staterooms, made impromptu material for much rapid-change dramatic performances, exquisitely absurd, and altogether entertaining. On we sped, with our jolly company, through New Jersey, rich and populous; on to Philadelphia, our great city neighbor, which, however, seems to most of us as far distant and unknown as Mars or the moon. Yet what a happy home place it is to those who dwell therein, and know the many advantages of its vast area, and consequent freedom from tenement drawbacks and other evils which we know too well. On we went through old Wilmington on the Delaware, with its red brick sidewalks and black lounging denizens; on through Baltimore, famous for good living and beautiful women; until in the afternoon we reached Washington and looked with admiration at the stately Capitol in the distance, with its splendid and graceful dome, and gazed with a sort of awe at the far-off Washington monument, that huge white obelisk, so gigantic, so spectral, so magnificent, but which is yet so chimney-like in its immensity as to be almost forbidding, if not revolting, to the æsthetic sense. I presume, though, that a nearer approach to the vast structure would overawe us with its colossal appearance. I have been told that the effect of that unbroken shaft near by, eighty feet wide at its base, and mounting skyward without a break, in perfect plainness, for five hundred and fifty-five

feet, is almost supernatural and overwhelming.
The very sight of the Capitol could not but bring
to our hearts the great crisis which was there im-
pending.   The huge dome seemed, as it were, to
cover in the great brain of the nation struggling
with the question, " Is America to engage in war ?
Is the nation which stands most for peace and
humanity to enter on a career of aggressive
arms ?"   It seemed an added wonder to our
" Flight in Spring " that we were entering thereon
at such a momentous time.   But life flows on in
many currents; and no matter what great crises
may occur in human affairs; duties, and even
pleasures, have each their place, and draw us after
them in either work or play.

II

On through the South.—Thomasville, Georgia.—Dr. Humphrey's Winter Home.—Southern Flowers.—The Old Plantation.—War Declared.—They Leave To-day.

SOON after leaving Washington the night came on, but ere darkness settled down upon us, we had already seen the fresh verdure, and the trees and flowers in full, radiant bloom.

Night closed in as we whirled on through the Southern land. We took the Atlantic Coast line, passing through many historic spots, well worth a stay; but our destination was Thomasville, Georgia, where we were to join our good host, Dr. Humphreys and his family, and rest with him at his winter home for a day or so, before starting on our full trip from New Orleans, by the Sunset Route, directly west, for Los Angeles.

Our stay in Thomasville was delightful. We found ourselves at home in the broad ample residence of our good host. The house is a large, one-story, double structure, standing in its own spacious grounds. A large hall, more than ninety feet long, runs through the midst of it. There we spent two days with our host, enjoying every moment of our stay. Flowers and roses were on every hand, and great trees with grateful shade, and the songs of many birds, and the pealing laughter of young folk, and the quiet happiness of those who loved to see others happy all about them.

The poetry and sentiment of the time, the place, the occasion, seemed to me to be symbolized in a lovely bouquet of wild flowers presented by Thomasville friends—Colonel and Mrs. Hammond—to our dear host and hostess, as a tender floral *bon voyage*. It was truly a thing of beauty in its rich and unstudied simplicity, made up of a great spray of wild pink azalea, and another of a flowering ash called Old Man's Beard. The silver threads of the latter fell over the exquisite color and finished form of the azalea, and all was overtopped by a branch of flaring crimson honeysuckle. It was both magnificent and dainty, all at once, and had the added beauty of most utter simplicity. It was merely a handful, plucked at random, from the abundant beauty of the rich Southern forest. I fancy, however, that an ordinary eye might have passed by the exquisite possibility of the Southern blooms, and that the unerring taste and tender sentiment of the givers were necessary factors in procuring such a perfect floral offering, so appropriate and so beautiful.

We had another great treat while at Thomasville, in a drive out to a Southern plantation of the old-time type. How sad and silent, though, it all seemed! It was like a charmed castle, waiting for the arrival of some one whose footsteps should quicken all to life again. There it stood, all ready for an awakened hospitality, at a moment's notice. We wandered through the great parlors, the spacious bedrooms, and out on the shaded balconies and verandas, peopling all, in imagination, with the home happiness for which it seemed so well prepared. The ample portico, with its great pillars; the luxuriant trees; the stately, silent house, and the tangle of roses and creeping plants made a picture long to be remembered. It did not seem quite right to romp and frolic in such a place, but such is the limit of our nature that one always loves and longs for contrasts; that is the reason, doubtless, why we awoke the echoes with many peals of ringing laughter and good fun. The ever-present kodak had its own share in our comedy, and brought away a shadow of our sport in the picture of "Rebekah at the Well."

The time came all too quickly for our departure from Thomasville. Even in our short stay we were charmed by the visits of many friends, among them some old acquaintances of other places and other times. We met, too, the genial editor of the "Daily Times-Enterprise," and found our departure duly mentioned in the issue of Saturday evening, April 16, 1898. It contained also the stupendous announcement of the certain opening of the war with Spain, which appeared in these startling head lines:

UNITED STATES ARMY ORDERED TO COAST

FIFTY THOUSAND VOLUNTEERS TO BE ORDERED OUT NEXT

SENATE STILL IN CONTINUOUS SESSION

But They Are Warming Up.—Money Calls Wellington a Liar.—The Queen Regent Contributes $200,000 to Equip Army and Navy.—Official Denial that European Powers Will Interfere.—Spain Says She Will Never Evacuate Cuba.— Uncle Sam Buying More War Ships.

Separated from the above, with the telegraphic detail following, was another head line which read:

"THEY LEAVE TO-DAY."

Any one would, on a hasty glance, suppose
that these words referred to the movements of
the United States army, but they did not; they
were spoken of *our departure*, on that afternoon,
for New Orleans and the Pacific Coast.   Here is
what followed the startling line, and as it intro-
duces our party in full and by name, we give it
in extenso:

"THEY LEAVE TO-DAY.

" Dr. Frederick Humphreys and his party will
leave to-day for an extended tour on the Pacific
Coast.

" The following is the *personnel* of the party:
Dr. and Mrs. Frederick Humphreys, the Misses
Hayden, Mr. J. F. Hanson, Rev. Dr. D. Parker
Morgan, of the Church of the Heavenly Rest,
New York, and Mrs. Morgan; Canon J. Harris
Knowles, of St. Chrysostom's, one of the Chap-
els of Trinity Church, New York; the Misses
Harding, of New York; Mr. Frank P. Payson
and Miss Sanford, of Brooklyn; and Miss Jayta
Humphreys and Mr. Frederick Humphreys, of
New York, the latter two being grandchildren of
Dr. and Mrs. Humphreys.

" All the party, except Dr. and Mrs. Humphreys, the Misses Hayden, and Mr. Hanson,

arrived here on Thursday, in the private car 'Lucania,' a palace on wheels, in which the tour will be made.

"Dr. Humphreys spent yesterday in showing his guests some of the attractive drives and scenery in and around the town. And they could not have had the guidance of one more familiar with this charming winter resort, or one more competent to tell of its many attractions. The good doctor has been a great friend of Thomasville, and all our people will cordially join us in the wish that he may spend many more happy winter months at his pretty home on Dawson Street. He has done much for the place, and it is duly appreciated by all classes of our citizens.

"The party will leave in the 'Lucania' this afternoon at 2.35. The itinerary will embrace the following principal points: New Orleans, San Antonio, El Paso, Los Angeles, San Diego, Santa Barbara, San Francisco, Monterey, San José, Ogden, Salt Lake City, Glenwood Springs, Colorado Springs, Denver, Kansas City, and St. Louis. Stops of more or less length will be made at all these points. New York will be reached on the 25th of May.

"It will be a most delightful, interesting, and instructive outing. We trust it may be made without a single mishap, and that the party may all reach their Northern homes in safety, and that when memory calls up its scenes and incidents,

Thomasville, clothed in its fresh garments of spring, with its countless flowers, its balmy air and blue skies, will have a place in the picture."

We can hear the cheery voice of our editorial friend, Captain Triplett, in all these lines, full of kindness and good feeling.

III

Departure from Thomasville.—Pet Superstitions.—Montgomery, Alabama.—The Capitol.—The Public Fountain.—Montgomery to New Orleans.

IT seemed as if we were commencing our journey in dead earnest as we were leaving Thomasville. Our party was complete, and we were all settled in our special places for the trip, our luggage and bags all in ship-shape order. The day, too, was Saturday, the 16th; hence our real beginning was not, after all, on the fatal " 13th," when we left New York. Some of us had little pet superstitions about numbers. Sixteen, however, seemed to satisfy all parties. It was composed of seven and nine, and had also in it two eights and four fours. Here was completeness and perfection, besides the mystery and infinity of the sacred seven and the thrice perfect nine.

On our way from New York, had we not also a bad omen? The end extension step of our car got ripped off at one of the stations; and as we were also shunted about a little at Thomasville, just before starting, rip went the other step. There was suppressed gloom at these accidents; but the said gloom was all dispersed when, some hours after, we were detained by a broken bridge. "There," said one of the ladies, "that is the third accident since we left. We are all safe now." Although the third accident was to a bridge, and not to our car, it, however, answered all purposes, and set us completely at rest.

How inevitable those little superstitions are, and how hard it is to despise them, or, as we say, rise above them! We sometimes laugh at them, but we cherish them all the same, and fain would show our more exalted wisdom by the mirth they give us. Unlucky days and numbers, together with signs and omens, and all such, are open questions with me. I should be sorry to be incapable of a little superstition, so called, now and then. Indeed, I rather believe it is all a phantasmal flickering of the abyss of mysteries with which we are, at all times and in all places, ever enveloped.

Off we are, then, from Thomasville, with waving handkerchiefs and pleasant farewells from the dear friends we leave behind. Our journey lay through a rich country, the whole effect like an

English landscape—luxuriant trees, and a verdant, undulating surface, glowing with flowers, and here and there, opulent with cultivation. We had hoped to have reached New Orleans in time for church service on Sunday morning, but the broken bridge prevented all that; and when we reached Montgomery, Alabama, we were too late, even there, for attendance at morning service, and were inexorably scheduled to leave for New Orleans early in the afternoon.

Our stay gave us an opportunity to get a sort of silent silhouette of the old Capitol of the Confederacy. A Sunday sleep was over the business portions of the town, broken only by the pathetic persistence of those who will run to the store, and look at the mail, or do something or other, from the mere fact that the average business man, in the average town, does not know what on earth to do with himself when not at work. He will hang around even on Sunday at his place of business, for it is less wearisome there than anywhere else.

Some of us saw at Montgomery the spot in the Capitol, marked by a star in the pavement, where Jefferson Davis stood when sworn in as President of the Confederacy; others of us in our stroll saw the public fountain, with its bronze tablets of:

2

"This side for colored people," "This side for white people," and also a tablet, of possibly universal application to blacks and whites alike: "No loafing round here." We also noticed a rather startling announcement at the Y. M. C. A. Hall: "The devil will be fought in four rounds here to-night."

Our afternoon and evening ride from Montgomery to New Orleans gave one the impression of all manner of possible wealth and progress. It seemed a rich, fertile country, needing but the influx of capital and labor to make it a paradise. There may be dragons lurking in swamps, or demons in the upper air, ready to hurl fiery darts at daring man in his Promethean efforts. But dragons can be starved by drainage, and atmospheric disturbances of storm and tornado, no doubt, do more good than harm in the long run.

It was well on in the night when we got into New Orleans, but we enjoyed the quiet of the Sunday, even on our speeding train. We felt the beauty of the great level stretches of flat land, mingled constantly with the gleaming waters of lake and bayou and morass, all looking more and more mysterious as the light faded away into the night.

IV

THE train moved along leisurely over bridges and trestle work, and through flowery forests, until, we scarcely knew how, we found ourselves at our temporary destination.

One could see very little of New Orleans in the short space of our stay, but we made the most of it. The city itself, in its historic and social aspects, is one of the most interesting in America and the least American. It has on it yet the traces of former Spanish and French ownership and occupation, but the equestrian statue of Old Hickory in Jackson Square, still known by its ancient name, the Place d'Armes, crowns all the past with the American idea. The monument of General Jackson is directly in front of the

Cathedral of St. Louis of France. We entered this edifice and noted the reredos back of the high altar, emblazoned with the arms of St. Louis and the record of his virtues.

While we were there, a large class of boys were being catechized, in the French tongue; again and again the answers would come in loud monotone. We noted, also, with interest, the unmistakable Gallic type, in head and eyes and hair, of the restless young scholars upon the benches.

Some of our party took carriage drives, and some preferred the ubiquitous street cars. In various ways we each sought our pleasure. We went to the cemeteries, with their overground, oven-like tombs, necessitated by the water-soaked condition of the soil. The French burial places had that sombre effect which straight lines and extended alleys ever produce. Why this disposition of line should so impress the mind is very curious, but I have always found it so. One feels it at Versailles, as well as in the most up-to-date of places, like Chicago. The vanishing points of long distances, where, as it were, one can never hope to reach, produce in the mind a kind of sorrow; while the curve, which conceals the unseen, urges on to pursue and attain to that which is beyond. Audubon Park, which we visited, and the Arboretum produce more pleasing effects by the winding walks and constant variety of beautiful trees and flowers. It is rather a doleful thing to make even the very best kept cemeteries places for lounging pleasure.

In the incongruity of such a situation, the frequent little green lizards flashing over the marble tombstones were a diversion. We caught one of them, and it was most curious to see it change color in its nervous alarm. From the most vivid green it became a dull blood red, and then brown, panting as if its heart would break; and not until it was well away from us did it return to its normal emerald tint.

It must be confessed that the ludicrous ever lurks near one in such places, and often, also, that which is sadder than sad. For instance, in the midst of the silent sombreness of the French cemeteries it was a dreary incident in the drama of life to see the placards of "For sale" on monuments whose occupation was gone, for they who were enclosed therein were, for some cause or another, to be ousted from their rest.

After we left the cemeteries some of our party had an *al fresco* lunch under some live-oak trees, where an honest German catered to our wants with the well-known products of the Fatherland. It was hot even there, but we wiled away an hour or so of rest in most satisfactory fashion.

We did the French market early in the morning, but possibly we were not early enough; for the whole place, display, and everything there seemed tame and commonplace. I found, however, pleasant study in some of the people, especially the poor, but aristocratic looking women with blue jean sunbonnets on, market baskets on their arms, and wearing dresses of most uncrinoline proportions.

We visited the new " St. Charles," where we all had dinner. The stay at this hotel brought back to mind the time, so long ago, when I first saw New Orleans. It was in January, 1870, shortly after the close of the War of the Rebellion. We were at the consecration of Bishop Pierce, at Mobile, Alabama, and visited New Orleans ere returning home. What memories came to me of the journey south through the historic battle-fields of the " Lost Cause"! I remember the long stretch of burnt locomotives standing on the tracks at Mobile; of Christ Church, where the consecration of Dr. Pierce was held, with its decoration of orange branches in fruit and flower; of the brilliant reception held

at the residence of our hostess, Mrs. Perry; and
the drawing-room, filled with flowers and elegantly
dressed women; while a wood fire, all aglow, gave
us a reminder that we must make believe it was
winter, because it was January.   Then there was
the steamboat ride from Mobile *via* Lake Pont-
chartrain, and thence to New Orleans.   The city
has changed much in these years.   We stayed
then at the old St. Charles, surely an old fire
trap, as events proved, but stately for all that.
The culmination of each day was the hotel dinner; and a daily parade, well worth seeing, was the
progress of the ladies across the huge rotunda,
through the lounging crowd, to the dining-room.
All that is now gone, and the new St. Charles
gets along without this primitive and, I must
say, pleasing display.

A memory also abides with me which I surely
may rehearse.   It was a dinner given to visiting ecclesiastics and lay dignitaries at the hospitable home of Dr. Mercer in Canal Street.
If I am right, he was a bachelor; he lived in
great elegance in his own house.   The dinner
was thoroughly Southern, and so intended.   I still
have pleasing reminiscences of the gumbo soup;
and a boned turkey, boiled, and stuffed with
oysters, ought not, and can not, ever be forgot-

ten.   It was pallid, but palatable, in its moist
modesty, and a cut right through its entire circumference was something to be brought away
as a grateful remembrance, safely disposed within
the inner man.

V

Impressions of New Orleans.—Its Harbor.—The Levee at
    Night.—Southern Texas.—Its Forests, Flowers, and
    Birds.—The Prairie Pool.

WE left New Orleans at 8.40 P.M., on Monday,
with visions of broad, unpaved streets embowered
in trees; of stately mansions in enclosed gardens;
of the huge levee, which, like a giant laid at
length, pushes its shoulders against the ever-
threatening flood of the mighty Mississippi. Our
ladies, too, had additional memories of the shopping districts; of ill-smelling open drains which
offended them; of ravishing summer goods of
cotton and silk from the looms of France; of exquisite bijouterie tempting to one's purse; of
great square paving blocks which seemed made to
float; and over all the remembrance of the yellow
flag of Spain, of the lily of France, and of the awakened bravery of the eagle of America, strangely
rousing up to war, and we hoped to conquest.

The great river at New Orleans is ever an

object of interest.   The huge three-sided bend which forms the harbor has a width varying from 1,500 to 3,000 feet, and a depth of from 60 to more than 200 feet.   This great body of water has at times a current of five miles an hour.   It is the aggregate of a river system extending more than 100,000 miles.   You may put together the Amazon, the Nile, the Ganges, and all the river systems of the earth, and they would scarcely approach the magnificent showing of the Father of Waters and its tributaries as it flows on by New Orleans to the sea.

As we looked back from our ferry-boat over the levee, luminous with its electric lights, at the huge bulk of the wonderful river over which we were passing, and then thought of all we had already seen in the few short days of our trip, and of all that was yet before us, we felt that rest in our dear " Lucania " would be welcome, and that we could well afford to sleep through Louisiana and wake in Texas.

When we woke up after our night's ride from New Orleans, we found ourselves in the southern part of that wondrous State, Texas.   One is not surprised that its vast extent should have awakened in its first adventurous settlers the dream of an independent " Lone Star Empire."   How could it be otherwise then, before the time and space annihilating forces of steam and electricity had been discovered and applied ? Now all is different. The great pulses of life and trade throb all through the world, in a wondrous fashion, of which our fathers could not even dream. Everywhere is now a centre to touch all else with influences.

It was lovely in the fresh morning light to look out over this jocund land. This is how it impressed dear Mrs. Morgan, and I transcribe directly from her diary, kindly placed at my disposal.

" Tuesday, April 19th.—Up early; a most exquisite morning. We pass through luxuriant forests of live oak, magnolia, and other trees of various kinds, draped in some places with southern moss, in others with beautiful creepers, among them the rich wistaria in full bloom.

" A heavy storm during the night left all the foliage sparkling with raindrops; and the songs of the birds and the odors from the refreshed earth added to the charm. It was a day of delight. Sat almost all the morning on the piazza in rear of the car in a state of beatitude.

" After the forest came sugar plantations—one of 5,000 acres, off which the owner last year made a million pounds of sugar. The cane, as we saw it, just coming up, resembled corn in its early

growth.   We also saw immense tracts of cotton,
and then came the prairie, a seemingly boundless expanse of green, gemmed with lovely wild
flowers.   There were acres of beautiful blue lark-
spur, crimson phlox, varieties of poppies, and
other yellow flowers, besides many that I failed
to recognize as we rushed along.   Here, too,
the mocking-birds perched on the wires and sang
to us, and the poet of the party was inspired to
write his lines on ' A Prairie Pool,' one of many
which we passed on our way."

I here give the little poem to which Mrs. Morgan refers.   The fatigues of the day before were
yet upon me, and I ensconced myself near one of
the windows to have a silent, quiet little spell all
to myself.   It was while thus abstracted, that
one of the many pools, left by the recent storm,
looked at me with its sunlit face and said as follows:

THE PRAIRIE POOL

Within my heart I hold the skies,
    Whatever hue they seem to wear ;
    In tempest gloom, or sunlight clear,
Their storm and shine alike I prize.

I lonely am, and motionless,
    And yet, what great things come to me !
    The planets in their mystery,
Sun, Moon, and Stars, the great, the less.

Deep in my heart I hold them all,
    Their quiring voices cheer my lot;
    All motionless in one lone spot,
Yet God's full heaven in sight and all.

And creatures great and creatures small,
    Find comfort in my fixed abode ;
    It may be man, or bird, or toad,
I share my life with each and all.

For all are dear to heart of God,
    And each can serve where'er he be ;
    Whether in life, full, rich, and free,
Or bound as I, by Prairie sod.

VI

AFTER a glorious day along the southern line
of Texas, at some points being very near the
Mexican frontier, we reached San Antonio at tea
time. Soon after, we were all ready, just in the
gloaming, for a leisurely stroll through the streets
of the beautiful and interesting town.

San Antonio had among its Spanish founders
some Jesuit missionaries, and these wise Fathers set
their Indian converts at once at good works which
took practical shape in the deep water courses
which still line the streets at each side to this
day, and bring to every man's door water for
irrigation, an absolute necessity in this dry climate. This accounts for the wealth of roses
which embower the trees and houses. It is a

paradise of sweet, flowery shrubs, and the air is vocal with the songs of the happy birds. "Never," says Mrs. Morgan in her diary, "Never have I heard such a wealth of bird music as here. Here, too, I first saw the Mexican red bird in its wild condition."

It has quite a charm to saunter round in a strange town, and mingle all unknown in the crowd. Thus we went in and out among them. The shops we found were attractive, especially those of the saddlers and harness makers, where the ingenious and practical shape of the goods, and their rich ornamentation in Mexican style, were quite interesting.

Just at dusk I entered the old Cathedral, a relic of Spanish times. The choir had in it the bishop's throne, and stalls for choristers. There were some paintings, also, which looked as if they might, in a better light, be worth seeing. But there was one thing there that possessed more interest than aught else. It was a body, waiting for burial, covered with a pall, and placed at the head of the centre aisle. It was a message from another world, a *memento mori*, which could not be thrust aside. How solemn it looked! and one thought of the long night watches, and of those who would remain by its side until the light of the next day should dawn, the Mass be said, and the grave receive the clay until the vivifying morning of the Resurrection.

Leaving the Cathedral we again mingled in the crowded streets, brilliant with electric lights, really now to be met with everywhere. In our stroll we saw the outside of the Alamo, which has quite a history. All had to wait, however, until next morning.

Here I may mention that our evenings on our car were always evenings at home. We had many a pleasant hour together in fun and frolic, in story-telling, in playing games, such as consequences and nonsense verses; in occasional singing, and music on the reed organ, part of our car belongings; but whatever we engaged in, we always brought our day to a close with family prayers and the singing of one or two hymns, as an act of devotion. When our closing hymn rang out from our car that night, at the depot grounds in San Antonio, doubtless many were curious to know just what we were. Since my return from our "Flight in Spring," it has occurred to me that much real pleasure and spiritual profit could be had by a mission band of clergymen making just such a tour as we made, but with the special end in view to hold services for one or more

days at the points visited.   I think the clergy
would hail such a mission with gladness, judging
from the hungry way in which Dr. Morgan and
myself were constantly importuned to " stay
over and preach."

One dear old brother made such a pitiful
appeal, and seemed so feeble, that Dr. Morgan
defied the injunction of his Vestry not to use his
throat while away, and disregarded even the
appealing advice of his dear wife, and did actually
preach.   The Doctor said that, of course, I would
do the same at night.   Of course, I had to consent.   Then a miracle took place: our dear old
brother seemed to have a new lease of life the
moment his two Sunday sermons were off his conscience.   He was so spry that on Sunday afternoon he suggested a Sabbath day's drive among
some orange groves, which we took behind two
spanking bays, the ribbons being held by our ere-
while feeble brother, now in all the vigor of
hearty old age, warming up to the exciting drive.
On and on we went until I suggested that it
would be well to turn back, as I wanted a little
quiet time before church to gather my thoughts
together before preaching.   In the blandest way
the old gentleman told us he had lost his way,
and was looking for a place to turn back.   I

thought we never should get home; but I made the best of it, and brooded all the return way on recent events at the Philippines, of Dewey and his watchword: "Keep cool and obey orders," and at night I gave a patriotic sermon on the text: "But thanks be to God which giveth us the victory."

I felt sure that if we remained over until next Sunday, our dear brother would be again as feeble as ever, and that in our charity we could not but preach, even though we might suspect. We did not leave San Antonio until after five o'clock the next day, and that gave us a little more pleasurable time there. It is such a flowery, bright, and cheerful place, that it quite attracted us.

In the morning I went to the Alamo and gave that thrilling place an hour or so, and it is well worth it. It has been the scene of a determined bravery of which any country might be proud, and there, also, a deep tragedy took place which has in it the true spirit of the daring and the heroic.

On the exterior the Alamo has quite an ancient appearance. The front, with its characteristic Spanish look and round-topped gable, is plain and massive, with quite a handsome entablature over the arched entrance, consisting of four fluted columns, on good bases, all supporting a horizontal cornice which extends over the main door,

and over a recessed niche at each side for statues.
It has all, a grandiose effect, quite interesting.

Passing in through the door, you find yourself
in a well-proportioned church, long since disused
as such, and now owned by the State and occupied as a museum, filled with relics of the fearful
scenes which took place within the sacred place.
Here, in the year 1836, a band of Texans fortified
themselves against the attack of General Santa
Anna and some four or five thousand Mexican
soldiers bent on their destruction.

The siege was laid, and the commanding officer
in the Alamo, Colonel Travis, determined to withstand it to the end. The same spirit filled the
hearts of his brave men. He endeavored to
arouse the energies of the Texans without to
come to his relief, but for some reason they did
not. Jealousies and bickerings among other lead-
ers is hinted at as the cause. The letter which
the brave colonel sent tells his story in his own
words. Here it is:

" COMMANDCY OF THE ALAMO, Bexar,
February 24, 1836.
" Fellow-Citizens and Compatriots : I am besieged by a thousand or more of the Mexicans
under Santa Anna. I have sustained a continued
bombardment for twenty-four hours, and have

not lost a man. The enemy have demanded a surrender at discretion; otherwise the garrison is to be put to the sword if the place is taken. I have answered the summons with a cannon shot, and our flag still waves proudly from the walls. *I shall never surrender or retreat.* Then I call on you in the name of liberty, of patriotism, and of everything dear to the American character, to come to our aid with all despatch. The enemy are receiving reinforcements daily, and will no doubt increase to three or four thousand in four or five days. Though this call may be neglected, I am determined to sustain myself as long as possible, and die like a soldier who forgets not what is due to his own honor and that of his country. Victory or death!

" W. BARRET TRAVIS,
" *Lieutenant-Colonel Commanding.*

" P. S.—The Lord is on our side. When the enemy appeared in sight we had not three bushels of corn. We have since found in deserted houses eighty or ninety bushels, and got into the walls twenty or thirty head of beeves.   T."

When the commandant issued this letter he had not accurate information of the exact strength of the besieging force, but it would have made no difference with such a man.

When the full power of the besiegers was known,

and the lines of attack became closer and closer, Colonel Travis assembled his men in the Alamo. Relief was not in sight, but the generous nature of Travis would not permit him to assign any other reason for this but the probability that his friends had been already cut off by the enemy.

After an impassioned speech to his men, referring to the failure to get relief, he thus concludes:

"Then we must die. Our business is not to make a fruitless effort to save our lives, but to choose the manner of our death. But three modes are presented to us. Let us choose that by which we may best serve our country. Shall we surrender, and be deliberately shot without taking the life of a single enemy? Shall we try to cut our way out through the Mexican ranks, and be butchered before we can kill twenty of our adversaries? I am opposed to either method. . . . Let us resolve to withstand our enemies to the last, and at each advance to kill as many of them as possible. And when at last they shall storm our fortress, let us kill them as they come! Kill them as they scale our walls! Kill them as they leap within! Kill them as they raise their weapons, and as they use them! Kill them as they kill our companions! and continue to kill them as long as one of us shall remain alive! . . . But leave every man to his own choice. Should any man prefer to surrender . . . or attempt to escape . . . he is at liberty to do so. My own choice is to stay in the fort and die for my country, fighting as long as breath shall remain in my body. This will I do even if you leave me alone. Do as you think best; but no man can die with me without affording me comfort in the hour of death."

The little pamphlet called " The Origin and Fall of the Alamo," which I bought within the walls, is my authority for what has preceded. I quote from it also the following simple, but telling story of what followed the speech of Colonel Travis:

" Col. Travis then drew his sword, and with the point traced a line upon the ground extending from the right to the left of the file. Then resuming his position in front of the centre, he said: ' I now want every man who is determined to stay here and die with me to come across that line. Who will be the first ? March!' The first respondent was Tapley Holland, who leaped the line at a bound, exclaiming, ' I am ready to die for my country!' His example was instantly followed by every man in the file, with exception of Rose——. Every sick man that could walk arose from his bunk, and tottered across the line. Col. Bowie, who could not leave his bed, said : ' Boys,

I am not able to come to you, but I wish some
of you would be so kind as to move my cot over
there.'   Four men instantly ran to the cot, and
each lifting a corner carried it over.   Then every
sick man that could not walk made the same request, and had his bunk moved in the same way.
   " Rose was deeply affected, but differently from
his companions.   He stood till every man but
himself had crossed the line.   He sank upon the
ground, covered his face, and yielded to his own
reflections.   A bright idea came to his relief;
he spoke the Mexican dialect very fluently, and
could he once get out of the fort, he might easily
pass for a Mexican and effect his escape.   He
directed a searching glance at the cot of Col.
Bowie.   Col. David Crockett was leaning over
the cot, conversing with its occupant in an under-
tone.   After a few seconds Bowie looked at Rose
and said : ' You seem not to be willing to die with
us, Rose.'   ' No,' said Rose, ' I am not prepared
to die, and shall not do so if I can avoid it.'
Then Crockett also looked at him, and said:
' You may as well conclude to die with us, old
man, for escape is impossible.'   Rose made no
reply, but looked at the top of the wall.   ' I have
often done worse than climb that wall,' thought
he.   Suiting the action to the thought, he sprang
up, seized his wallet of unwashed clothes, and
ascended the wall.   Standing on its top, he looked
down within to take a last view of his dying

friends. They were all now in motion, but what they were doing he heeded not; overpowered by his feelings, he looked away, and saw them no more. . . . He threw down his wallet, and leaped after it."

I will now let the Mexicans tell how they made the attack and also the result to them, giving extracts from official documents and from the recital of Sergeant Becerra, a Mexican:

" A terrible fire belched from the interior. Men fell from the scaling ladders by the score, many pierced through the head by balls, others felled by clubbed guns. The dead and wounded covered the ground. After half an hour of fierce conflict, after the sacrifice of many lives, the column of Gen. Castrillon succeeded in making a lodgment in the upper part of the Alamo to the northeast. It was a sort of outwork. This seeming advantage was a mere prelude to the desperate struggle which ensued. The doors of the Alamo building were barricaded by bags of sand as high as the neck of a man; the windows also. On top of the roofs of the different apartments were rows of sand bags to cover the besieged.

" Our troops [the Mexicans], inspired by success, continued the attack with energy and boldness. The Texians fought like devils. It was at short range—muzzle to muzzle, hand to hand, musket and rifle, bayonet and bowie-knife—all were mingled in confusion. Here a squad of Mexicans, here a Texian or two. The crash of firearms, the shouts of defiance, the cries of the dying and wounded made a din almost infernal. The Texians defended desperately every inch of the fort; overpowered by numbers they would be forced to abandon a room. They would rally in the next, and defend it until further resistance became impossible.

" Gen. Tolza's command forced an entrance at the door of the church building. He met the same determined resistance without and within. He won by force of numbers and great sacrifice of life.

" There was a long room on the ground floor. It was darkened. Here the fight was bloody. It proved to be the hospital. A detachment of which I had command had captured a piece of artillery. It was placed near the door of the hospital, doubly charged with grape and canister, and fired twice. We entered and found the corpses of fifteen Texians. On the outside we afterwards found forty-two dead Mexicans.

" On the top of the church building I saw eleven Texians. They had some small pieces of artillery and were firing on the cavalry and on those engaged in making the escalade. Their ammunition was exhausted, and they were loading with pieces of iron and nails.

" The Alamo was entered at daylight; the fight did not cease till nine o'clock. . . .

" Gen. Santa Anna directed Col. Mora to send out his cavalry to bring in wood. This was done. The bodies of the heroic Texians were burned. Their remains became offensive. They were afterward collected and buried by Col. Juan N. Seguin."

Sergeant Becerra said:

" There was an order to gather our own dead and wounded. It was a fearful sight. Our life-less soldiers covered the ground surrounding the Alamo. They were heaped inside the fortress. Blood and brains covered the earth and the floors, and had spattered the walls. The ghastly faces of our comrades met our gaze, and we removed them with despondent hearts. Our loss in front of the Alamo was represented at two thousand killed, and more than three hundred wounded. The killed were generally struck on the head. The wounds were in the neck or shoulder, seldom below that. The firing of the besieged was fear-fully precise. When a Texas rifle was levelled on a Mexican, he was considered as good as dead. All this indicated the dauntless bravery and the cool self-possession of the men who were engaged in a hopeless conflict with an enemy numbering more than twenty to one. They inflicted on us a loss ten times greater than they sustained. The

victory of the Alamo was dearly bought. Indeed, the price in the end was well-nigh the ruin
of Mexico."

The tragic heroism displayed in the Alamo
caused intense excitement in the United States,
and, indeed, throughout the civilized world.
Lovers of liberty knew that the men were inspired
both by their love of freedom and the consciousness of the horrible fate which would await them
if they fell alive into the hands of Santa Anna and
his men. The pamphlet tells us that :

" An Englishman named Nagle had the honor
of originating the ' Monument Erected to the
Heroes of the Alamo.' It stood at the entrance
of the Capitol at Austin. This building was
burned in 1880, and the monument suffered in-
jury. On the top of each front were the names
of Travis, Bowie, Crockett, and Bonham. The
inscription on the north front was: ' To The God
Of The Fearless And The Free Is Dedicated This
Altar Of The ALAMO.' On the west front:
' Blood of Heroes Hath Stained Me. Let The
Stones Of The Alamo Speak, That Their IMMO-
LATION Be Not FORGOTTEN.' On the
south front: ' Be They Enrolled With LEONI-
DAS In The Host Of The Mighty Dead.' On
the east front: ' Thermopylæ Had Her Messenger
Of DEFEAT, But The ALAMO Had None.' "

After seeing the Alamo and penetrating its historic recesses, I was in no mood for much further sightseeing. Some of our party drove to a most interesting Mission on the outskirts of the town, others contented themselves with a distant view of it from the street cars. The weather was too hot for much further exertion, and it was with a sense of restful enjoyment that we reclined in our car " Lucania " as we speeded westward in the evening hour. We got a charming view of San Antonio, a mile or so out from the town, glowing in the radiance of the setting sun, and looking as neat, thriving, and attractive as we found it in our experience. It seemed to deserve the added splendor of the sunset glow; and as a light of historic glory, and of a fame which can never set, we here insert a few striking lines called the " Hymn of the Alamo."

HYMN OF THE ALAMO

By Captain Reuben M. Potter, U.S.A.

Rise ! man the wall—our clarion's blast
   Now sounds the final reveille ;
This dawning morn must be the last
   Our fated band shall ever see.
To life, but not to hope, farewell ;
   Your trumpet's clang, and cannon's peal,
And storming shout, and clash of steel
   Is ours, but not our country's knell.

Welcome the Spartan's death—
 'Tis no despairing strife—
We fall—we die—but our expiring breath
 Is Freedom's breath of life.

" Here on this new Thermopylæ
 Our monument shall tower on high,
And ' Alamo ' hereafter be
 On bloodier fields the battle cry."
Thus Travis from the rampart cried.
 And when his warriors saw the foe
Like whelming billows move below,
 At once each dauntless heart replied :
" Welcome the Spartan's death—
 'Tis no despairing strife—
We fall—we die—but our expiring breath
 Is Freedom's breath of life ! "

They come—like autumn leaves they fall,
 Yet hordes on hordes they onward rush ;
With gory tramp they mount the wall,
 Till numbers the defenders crush.
The last was felled—the fight to gain—
 Well may the ruffians quake to tell
How Travis and his hundred fell
 Amid a thousand foemen slain.
They died the Spartan's death,
 But not in hopeless strife ;
Like brothers died—and their expiring breath
 Was freedom's breath of life.

Among the many pleasant incidents of our stay in San Antonio was the meeting with some of the students of the West Texas Military Academy, of which my young friend the Rev. A. L. Burleson is the rector. They were splendid young fellows. It was a regret that I could not visit the school and pay my respects to one who bears the honored name of Burleson.

To look at those young students was a delight; and to know that the seed sown at Racine, under De Koven, where the Rev. Mr. Burleson graduated, was here, in this great Southwest, bearing such good fruitage, was a delightful memory to bring away from San Antonio.

VII

AFTER leaving San Antonio, the night soon shut
out the landscape from our view, and the next
morning revealed to us a rather forlorn region.
This is how it impressed Mrs. Morgan. I quote
from her diary: " We awoke to find ourselves in
a desolate portion of country, bare prairie, stretching away towards craggy hills whose irregular out-
line is very picturesque, and the soft blue and
purple shadowing on them is beautiful. Droves
of cattle wandered about, feeding on the sparse
dried grass, which is the only forage the poor
beasts seem to have."

Even the most unpromising places have some

compensation in them, for the beauty of the distant mountains was worth seeing, and the natural cured grass of the prairies has wonderful sustaining power. In fact, it is a hay crop wisely scattered everywhere, needing neither storehouse nor barn, always on hand—or at mouth, one might say—for the strolling droves. We passed during our morning's run some splendid pieces of railroad engineering. We were constantly rising above the sea level, every mile bringing us up to the mountain heights. This rapid ascent was managed by a most circuitous route among the foothills, winding in and out, and doubling again and again upon our track. A railway map gives one an idea of almost straight lines from place to place. How different is the reality! It seemed to me a symbol of theory and practice in real life. A proposition in business or in morals seems as simple and inevitable as that two and two make four; but many are the twists and turns that must be taken in all departments of life before the end in view can be attained.

By these necessary zigzags and retracing curves we made our advance, higher and higher. The sparse vegetation revealed our increasing altitude, the trees became few and stunted, and the wild plants more limited in variety. We descend again as we pass on, until toward evening we reached El Paso. Here we landed in the midst of a fearful sand storm. We were met by a dear old friend of former days, the Rev. Dr. Higgins, whose first impulse was to tell us that it was not always thus in El Paso. We should hope not; for it was fearful. The wind blew at a dreadful rate, sweeping along with it dense clouds of sharp sand which gave one a sense of being lashed with whipcords. In the midst of this blinding dust and sand, obscuring the light, people moved about like huge grasshoppers. A contrivance of transparent celluloid, fitted like glasses to the eyes, extending from above the eyebrows, down well on the cheeks, gave people this absurd insect-like appearance. It was gruesome and comical at once. Several of our party invested immediately in these most necessary appliances, in order to get round a little in what looked like a forlorn town; but ere an hour or so had passed we found the storm gone, and all in placid peace, while the stars shone down through the clear night with true southern brilliancy.

The next morning Dr. Higgins was once more with us, and was delighted to act as guide to our younger contingent, who did El Paso thoroughly, and went also across the river, the Rio Grande del

Norte, into the Mexican town of Juarez. Some of the party met with a sad experience on their return, when they had to pay so much a pound tax, and *ad valorem* besides, on a Mexican blanket whose gay stripes had taken their fancy in a shop at Juarez.

My cicerone was the Rev. M. Cabell Martin, Rector of St. Clement's, El Paso, who drove me in his buggy over the frontier to Juarez and showed me all that was to be seen. It is astonishing what a change one sees in little more than a few yards of distance. Once across the bridge from El Paso, and you are in a new atmosphere. El Paso is like a New England town, after all; a little rough here and there, a little strange it may be, like the strangeness of the city pets, the alligators, who sleep in luxurious laziness in the public square; but yet it all was in our ways, and we were at home. But in Juarez all is different. As we drive along, two men by the roadside making adobe looked as if they might have been with the Israelites in Egypt at the same business. With their naked legs they were kneading up the black muck, which, when of the proper consistency, they deftly moulded into form for the great master workman, the sun, to dry at his leisure and pleasure. The streets of the town seemed bare.

The shops were in most cases without windows or exterior openings, save the entrance door. The booths and stalls in the streets for cheap eatables, vegetables, pottery, and odds and ends had a wild, gypsy grace about them, all water-colors, ready to be painted, just as they were.

We saw the post-office where Juarez kept up the government and existence of the Republic of Mexico during the whole of the Maximilian invasion. It was a close point to the United States for escape and liberty if he was molested. When Maximilian received his death-shot, Juarez went on with his presidency, taking no notice whatever of the usurpation as if it never had place. This man, of pure Indian blood, was certainly of heroic mould, and a stanch lover of light and liberty.

We looked into the church, a most interesting old adobe building, with walls of immense thickness. The interior was a well-proportioned parallelogram of good height, with a grand wooden roof of carved beams of a dark hue, possibly black with age. We were told that the work had been all done by native workmen in ages past. Part of the doors in the same style, like Aztec work, had been ripped away and thrown outside to make way for a jimcrack gallery for singers. We longed to bring those old doorposts with us, and looked up with gratification at the roof as yet safe in its distance and old magnificence. The church walls had been all done up in whitewash, and the altar was adorned with saints and a Madonna decked out in real laces, satins, velvets, and jewelry, possibly real also. The effect of it all was bizarre and a trifle depressing.

We saw the arena for the Sunday and *fête*-day bull fights, and also the square behind the church where the Mexican padre indulges in his form of church sociables and grab-bag business. He does it by letting out the spaces of the square to all sorts of three-card-monte men, and other catch-pennies of that ilk, from December 8th, through the Christmas Holidays, until the following *fête* of the Epiphany. It is said that the padre gets his percentage on the profits also. Poor man, he must have some compensation, for his lot is such that, under the laws of Mexico, he, or any other padre, cannot walk the streets in clerical garb, but must disguise their calling in the ordinary dress of a civilian. The padre in question, I was told, usually appeared in the dress of an ordinary peon.

We took a peep into the prison, and were instantly assailed by the prisoners behind the bars and in the open court within the gates, offering us for sale trinkets they had made. The Mexican prison rules do not oblige the jailers to provide food for their prisoners, so they must in some way hustle for themselves, buy from their jailers, or depend upon the charity of others. An officer in full uniform lounged on a chair near by the outer door, and soldiers in canvas uniforms were on guard with military rigidity, with arms in their hands. It was like a bit out of the Middle Ages, or a scene from the opera, where brigands and regulars have varying fortunes of conquering and being conquered.

It was nice to drive back over the Rio Grande del Norte again into the home land; to have a chat with the United States Custom House officer; to show him our purchases worth about fifty cents American money, for which we had got eight or ten pieces of pottery from a street vender, and then after our chat to be told " it was all right."

When we got into El Paso we saw the first touch of real war in the shape of a regiment of cavalry bound for New Orleans and Cuba. There were shouts and hurrahs as they moved off in their train, but not the noisy enthusiasm which one might expect. Our American people are not shouters, they are too serious. There is a silence about their most excited conditions which a stranger can hardly understand.

VIII

WE left El Paso with pleasant recollections of
all the kindness we received there, and once again
we travelled into the night. Ere that, however,
we had ample time to note the rapidly increasing
desert character of our surroundings. The whole
thing was like a Salvator Rosa setting for wild
adventure and daring lawlessness. I am confident
that any one owning a horse there, and not over-
burdened with moral sense, would almost unconsciously become a desperado. May we not
imagine that man is apt to develop within himself
the characteristics of those animals who find a
subsistence in such places ? There the sly coyote,
the panther, and wildcat inhabit; there, too, the
rattlesnake and other venomous things have their
life; and may not the environment which produces

such creatures have like effect upon men who grow up or dwell there? Such were my reflections when at Deming, where we made a wait of twenty minutes, I saw an armed guard mount our train to be all ready for possible train robbers. One of the guards was a sweet-looking, mild-mannered man, quite young; but the conductor told me that that sweet fellow was the one who did the business, by a sure shot, in the last recent train-robbing escapade. It seemed all a matter of course, to fit in nicely with the landscape, and did not trouble us in the least nor disturb our tranquil rest. The morning found us all safe and unmolested, which was rather a disappointment to some of our ladies who wished especially to encounter a train robbery or hold-up. The ideal highwayman is ever held to be gallant to the ladies, even when depriving them in good old-fashioned way of their jewels.

The desert of Arizona, through which we were speeding, had the same pale and tawny look of dry, rocky, and alkaline soil; but nature is never idle anywhere. Here we were entertained with whirling processions of immense cacti, some thirty feet high, which seemed to dance past us in grim, grotesque fashion as we rode along. Some species were gorgeous in blood-red blossoms, an admirable contrast to the pale, bell-shaped flowers of the yucca plant.

At Yuma we had a vivid evidence of what care and irrigation can do even in this arid waste. The station enclosure was a mass of brilliant beauty. There were red, pink, and white oleanders. There were pomegranates in full bloom, with their rich yellow blossoms.

An enthusiastic German whom I met was quite enraptured with the sight of palms and flowers, and declared that the railroad company ought to establish oases such as this, but larger, at frequent intervals, well furnished with casinoes, music, hotels, and all the appliances of Monte Carlo. One can imagine that in this perfect air, and with such luxurious surroundings, a lotos sort of life might be enjoyed for a resting spell now and then.

The platform of the station was lined up with Indians having various trinkets for sale, more or less authentic. The rich tint of the Indian complexion, especially among the younger women and children, exactly harmonized with the bright light and vivid surroundings of the desert beyond and the flowers near by.

There was a graceful Indian Madonna there, with her chubby baby boy, that any artist might

covet to paint. Our kodaks were unable to snap
them off, for the moment the drop of the camera
was on them the Indian mothers gathered their
brood under their shawls and wraps, just as a hen
would gather her chickens under her wings from a
hawk. There is a widespread superstition among
primitive people that some evil may be wrought
to a person by working enchantment upon his or
her likeness or image. This is fearfully brought
out in Dante Gabriel Rossetti's poem, "Sister
Helen." The poet discovers to us, in some ancient castle, Sister Helen and her little brother.
The child speaks and the sister replies in this
fashion:

"Why do you melt your waxen man,
      Sister Helen?
  To-day is the third since you began."
"The time was long, yet the time ran,
      Little brother."
    (*O Mother, Mary Mother,*
Three days to-day, between Hell and Heaven!)

"But if you have done your work aright,
      Sister Helen,
  You'll let me play, for you said I might."
"Be very still in your play to-night,
      Little brother."
    (*O Mother, Mary Mother,*
Third night, to-night, between Hell and Heaven!)

" You said it must melt ere vesper bell,
    Sister Helen ;
  If now it be molten, all is well."
" Even so,—nay, peace ! you cannot tell,
    Little brother."
    (O Mother, Mary Mother,
O what is this, between Hell and Heaven !)

In this weird fashion the poem moves along.
The whole story of the wronged Sister Helen and
her false lover, upon whose waxen image she
works her spell, is told us, until at last, the waxen
image consumed, the child with his pure, innocent
eyes sees the wraith of the dead man cross the
threshold of the apartment where they are. The
child exclaims :

" See, see, the wax has dropped from its place,
    Sister Helen,
  And the flames are running up apace."
" Yet here they burn but for a space,
    Little brother !"
    (O Mother, Mary Mother,
Here for a space, between Hell and Heaven !)

" Ah ! what white thing at the door has cross'd,
    Sister Helen ?
  Ah ! what is this that sighs in the frost ? "
" A soul that's lost as mine is lost,
    Little brother !"
    (O Mother, Mary Mother,
Lost, lost, all lost, between Hell and Heaven !)

As we looked at the Indian women cuddling up their babes from the shot of the camera, we saw an evidence of those deep and widespread superstitions which make the whole world kin.

After leaving Yuma we soon cross the Colorado River, and ere darkness set in upon us we could see the ordered lines of vines and olives, of apricots and oranges, in rich and cultivated California, whose many wonders both of nature and of man were soon to open more fully before us.

IX

WE reached Los Angeles at nightfall, and it was a fitting entrance to that enchanted spot. Through the shadows, as we approached, we caught glimpses of the beauties that awaited us when light should dawn.

The station was bright and cheerful, and the anchorage for our car was in a delightsome spot, withdrawn in a garden from the noise and confusion so inevitable in the regions of the iron horse. Night as it was, we made a little tour of inspection ere turning in for sleep. Emerging from the depot, the first thing that confronted us was a giant palm, towering up in the darkness of the night, yet glowing with electric light, which brought out its tropical foliage splendidly. Its graceful and splendid form made a beautiful initial letter to the bewitching chapter which Los Angeles presented for our future inspection.

Sunday morning came to us in our smiling garden like a benediction. The place was small in itself, but so well laid out that it had the full effect of spaciousness. It was glowing with roses, pansies, stocks, and any number of other flowers. A gorgeous bordering of a species of ice plant with splendid magenta blooms was especially effective. All this profusion was accented by beautiful trees—the pepper-tree, the red gum, and several species of palm. There was also near by a collection of Arizona plants in all their grotesque shapes, and a most interesting group of hieroglyphic rocks brought from some mountain place, having on them prehistoric inscriptions of lines and rude figures, suggesting the Ogham records found in Ireland and other parts of Europe, usually attributed to most primitive times.

It was my privilege to assist at the service at St. Paul's Church, where the Bishop of Los Angeles preached. The unwinterish conditions of this climate were well suggested by the out-of-door passage of choir and clergy from the choir-room to the church. The service was well rendered by a choir of men and boys. In the evening it was my lot to preach. It was delightful to join in the worship of the Church, and to be as much at home among brethren on the shores of the Pacific as if we were thousands of miles away, on the other side of the continent, near another sea. We spent our next day at Los Angeles and neighborhood in democratic fashion, going by street and electric cars in various directions. We went out to Pasadena, where a Chicago friend gave us a pressing invitation to stay over and visit his villa built on the old Spanish model. His kind hospitality, so hearty and unexpected, we could not accept. We had, like most tourists, to press on. Now California, of all places, is a region to tarry in. It is too huge, too complicated, too strange to be done in a flying visit, although a flying visit is well worth having. The clear atmosphere makes you imagine you could take an easy stroll over to the mountains, but a day would not suffice to reach them. You think you have exhausted some place or other, but you find that you have only skimmed over the surface.

We left Los Angeles with regret in the afternoon of our third day there. We were sorry to leave our pretty garden anchorage, where we had for a near neighbor the distinguished Madam Melba, travelling on a concert tour in her private car. The diva had quite a suite in attendance.

The only music that we heard from its sacred interior was from her colored *chef*, who, while his mistress was on the concert stage, made the garden, where we were wandering about in the moonlight, vocal with her piano and his by no means unmelodious voice. There was a touch of the comic in this sentimental proceeding quite irresistible.

Our memory of Los Angeles and the whole *entourage* of that garden spot will always be a vision of palms and flowers, of beautiful homes embowered in roses, of orange-trees in fruit and flower, and of a far-extended city whose future must be as magnificent as its present is beautiful.

We spent a delightful afternoon on our journey southward from Los Angeles to San Diego and Coronado Beach. We passed through the distinctive orange belt of Southern California, and the golden fruit was in evidence on every hand. Oranges lay on the ground. The groves were like gardens of the Hesperides with glittering yellow fruit for all mankind. They were ready in trains side-tracked for transhipment across the continent; they were in warehouses, where we could see through the great open doors the busy packers at their work; they were everywhere, until the eye almost tired of them, and the formal rows of the orange groves, and the bare earth underneath always kept ploughed up for advantage to the coveted crop. In other places we passed enormous herds of cattle, fat and well liking, giving one an idea of the huge proportions of ranch life on this great Pacific Coast.

Our route brought us for the first time really close to the great ocean which we had never seen. When one comes on the first view of any great object there is always a thrill of expectancy. We had left the great Atlantic behind us, and we were speeding on rapidly to the shores of the Pacific. We knew that in a few moments it would burst upon our sight, but just then a dense, soft, and chilling fog surrounded us. It seemed a great disappointment to have such a hindrance to our sight just at that time; but, it was all for the best, as we soon discovered; for when we did see the mighty deep, nothing could be more sublime than its veiled magnificence. There was a fog, it was true, but it was a vast veil of pearl-tinted tissue, and out of it rolled the huge breakers, like giants at play, whose locks were white as wool, and their great pale arms entwined in majestic sport.

We were passing on high bluffs close to the shore. The curious and precipitous clay banks were worn into fantastic shapes.   Here and there we could see, far down, fishermen's huts and settlements, and occasional villages.   Oil wells, also, with their hideous cranes and well machinery closely jostled together in eager greed, offended our sense of the picturesque, with their uncompromising utility; but on and beyond all was the mighty deep, muffled by the mist, and looking more mysterious and magnificent with its great dashing breakers than if we were viewing it under the light of the brightest day.

With the attendant symphony of this deep shrouded sea, we reached San Diego.

X

OUR ride of four hours from Los Angeles to
San Diego was rather warm, and after our arrival
we cared to do little more than lounge about the
station in the evening. Near by was a most inviting bathing-house, beautifully fitted up with
all sorts of appliances for comfort, not the least
of these being a superb swimming-pool, whose
tempered waters were sending to us insinuating
invitations to take a good plunge and enjoy the
charms of their dark, silent depths. It was too
soon after eating, and we put it all off until next
day.

When we men folk returned to our car from
the adjacent bath-house, a feeling of gloom and
melancholy settled down upon us. The "Lucania" was silent and lonely, save for the ser-

vants.   Not another soul was visible.   The ladies had all disappeared!

Here was an alarming state of affairs.   Those who had wives, were as though they had them not, and those who had not wives, were as though they had.   We were all alike disturbed and miserable at the unaccountable absence of our better halves.   What had become of them ?   We seemed to be quite on the outskirts of San Diego.   The wide streets, stretching away in darkness, looked terrible and forbidding.   Who could tell what desperado might not have made away with them ?   It would be a mere matter of a sudden stoop down from a horse, perhaps, a seizure by a pair of strong arms, a wild ride over the boundless plain, and misery would settle down upon us as another mysterious disappearance had to be recorded, and remain possibly forever unexplained.   We called a council of war, so to speak.   We determined to investigate, and boldly plunged into the unknown town in search of our lost ones.   Every man we met had the possibilities in him, to our excited imaginations, of a double-dyed cut-throat; every saloon was a gate of Hades; but we bravely pushed on.   We found ourselves soon in rather an attractive street.   Shops were gay with life.   The ever-present electric lamps gave us their cold glitter and their fantastic shadows, until at last, joyful sight, we saw all our ladies shopping to their hearts' content in a Chinese curio shop, where a great, bland, round-faced Chinaman, like a six-foot baby, was all smiles and attention to the purchasing crowd. We joined them as if nothing had happened, and remained with them until we saw them safe back. All the preceding is summed up in one of the ladies' diaries briefly thus: " We arrived at San Diego at 6 P.M. After tea the ladies of the party started out to *see the town*, visited two curio shops, and went back to the car before nine, and received a very severe scolding for going off by ourselves." The italics in the above are mine.

I think the ladies served us right, for we should have awaited their pleasure; but who could have dreamed that they wanted to do anything more than rest after their fatiguing ride ?

The comical side of the whole thing is this: that our ladies, in their little independent cruise in San Diego, were as safe as if they were in any Eastern village. San Diego is, in fact, a typical American town of the better class, nurtured by Boston capital, so largely invested in stock of the Santa Fé Railroad, whose western terminus is at San Diego, which is also peopled by New Englanders, who have duly brought with them to the Pacific Slope, a full and perennial supply of their steady habits.

In our one full day in San Diego we saw much to interest us. A carriage drive took some of us over Mission Cliffs, others went round in the great, double-decked tram cars, and all took in the vast extent of San Diego, as it lies on a huge, sloping shelf over the Pacific, giving constant prospects of the mountains and the sea. We also visited Coronado, the city so called, the beach, and the hotel. The city, on the great peninsula between San Diego Bay, a beautiful expanse of water, and the great ocean beyond, has, of course, what every Western effort has—a future.

The beach, where the great rollers of the Pacific dash in, was magnificent; but one cannot safely bathe thereon. The water is heroically cold, and the surf too fierce and heavy for ordinary mortals. The sea water, warmed, tamed, and confined in a bath-house, is what is safest to take.

I quite sympathized with one of our ladies who declared to me that she was never more disappointed in her life than with the beach at Coronado. "Why," said she, " I thought I could gather shells and sea-weed, and pick pretty pebbles; but there is nothing." Well, she was right in a sense. Perhaps it was because that particular spot was harried over and over by visitors *à la* Coney Island, so that it was bare of all those curious things " cast up by the sea;" or perhaps it was that the huge surf constantly tumbling in raises the sand perpetually, and buries all objects, whatever they may be, rapidly out of sight.

One of our party, who wished to improve the occasion and also give me a treat, paid fifty cents a piece for himself and myself to gain admission to a museum on the beach, said to be a wonderful collection of interesting things in natural history.

I noticed rather a startled look upon the lady caretaker's face as the money was paid. I may here say we found the doors open and a sign at the entrance giving price of admission. We might have pushed in without the formality of a cash payment, but the dignity of our cloth forbade. My friend really made an effort to summon the caretaker from some inner recess. She took our money—his money, I should say—with a startled air, and we entered.

Well, the less said the better about that museum. No wonder that our payment to get in was startling. We who had seen Kensington, the Crystal Palace at Sydenham, the British Museum, the World's Fair, and about one hundred and twenty

years of life between us, were greeted with shabby
plaster reproductions of this, that, and the other;
with jute-haired, manufactured monsters and other
absurdities; the only thing that really commanded
our respect being an American coon tolerably
well stuffed and set up. We left disgusted. My
reflection to my friend was that in such localities
the best things were always " free shows," as I
pointed out to the boundless Pacific; the hard,
firm sand of the beach; and

" The white arms out in the breakers, tirelessly tossing."

But the melancholy of the museum had yet an
outside chapter, for there were cages of wild
beasts—miserable captives—and some wretched
monkeys, whose capacity for the pathetic grief
which was stamped upon their poor faces, turned
one's thoughts inward to the tragedy of all life.

The hotel was one of the many " largest hotels
in the world," and is really a wonderful place.
The great interior court, with glass roof covering
in a collection of tropical trees and plants, was all
a thing of beauty. Into this magic place quite a
number of rooms opened. The dining-room, the
ballroom, the verandas, the sun-parlors, the public rooms—all were vast, grandiose, and what one

might say "perfectly splendid." I pity the taste of any one who could stand all this splendor, with its crowds of people, for any length of time. It seemed rather deserted when we were there; too late for one season, too early for another. This, and a certain shabby want of repair here and there, made the place seem somewhat sad. It is no easy matter to keep up a show place of such huge extent, with the hungry air of the great Pacific ever whetting its teeth upon every atom of its vast and profusely ornamented surface.

While at San Diego, we noticed a weird effect common on the Pacific Coast, resulting from certain curious atmospheric conditions. The heavens at times are hung with a great veil of what is called "high fog." This bank of vapor shuts out all the upper sky. Between it and the earth is a stratum of hot, dry air, down through which the collected moisture above can never descend. It has to float off to the distant mountains. It has to be caught by their rocky arms, and turned into rain or snow, and then descend as rivers to the dry and dusty plains beneath.

When we were starting out on our carriage ride in the morning, as I noticed this lowering mass of vapor above us, I asked the driver if it was going to rain. "Lord," said he, with an amused and bored shrug, '' it will not rain here until next November!'' It must have a queer effect upon people to be constantly held in the vise of such inevitable and square-cut atmospheric influences as these.

San Diego to Santa Barbara.—The Old Mission.—The
Inner Cloister.—The Afternoon Ride.—The Lady of
the Blue Jeans.—Samarcand.

OUR car moved off from San Diego in the early
morning, before breakfast. We enjoyed that meal
en route for Los Angeles, returning there by
the way we came. After a delay of a few hours
in the lovely city of rose-covered homes and em-
bowering trees, we began our journey to Santa
Barbara, which we reached well on into the evening. Our course brought us soon again to the
ever-attractive shores of the great tossing ocean,
ever full of mystery, and provocative of brooding
thoughts.

When we arrived at Santa Barbara, it was toward
evening, so tea and a stroll filled up the close of
our day of travel.

The next morning found us ready for a full day
of what turned out to be exquisite pleasure. A
drive to the old Mission of Santa Barbara, with

a prolonged stay within the charmed shade of the old cloister, filled the forenoon.

The antiquity of more than a hundred years seems an eternity in such a new land as this, and hence the old mission seemed old indeed; but it had the lustre of the dim past also, for our guide was a monk of St. Francis, and his religious dress carried us back for over six centuries to sunny Italy and the cradle of his order, Assisi, where St. Francis dwelt.

Santa Barbara Mission is one of the best preserved of the many old Spanish religious settlements yet remaining in Southern California, and its style gives the norm of all the rest. It has a certain grandiose air suggestive of Spanish magnificence, and reminds one of those stately creatures one meets so often in Spain, who ask for alms with high-toned elegance, and return thanks with the manners of a prince. Such was Santa Barbara. Before the chief entrance of the chapel was a grand flight of steps, with a generous platform capable of giving standing-room to any church ceremonial or gathering of worshippers. It was made up, it is true, of small mason work and stucco; but the effect was there, and that effect was good. Entering the chapel, we found ourselves in a stately, flat-roofed building of con-

siderable height and length.   There were several
altars at each side, and a number of religious pictures, quite of the Murillo school, and a Pieta in
plaster, just as one finds Michael Angelo's great
masterpiece in St. Peter's.   Beyond all, was the
high altar, rather poor and shabby, but pathetic,
nevertheless, in its earnest purpose, with its hang-
ing lamp telling of the Sacramental Presence
within the Tabernacle.   The tomb of the first
Roman Catholic bishop of California is at the
Epistle side of the altar; and close by, on the outside, are other graves.

A lay brother took us all over the place.   We
rang for him at the entrance door in the cloisters,
and found him a sweet-faced, cheerful, humble
man, delighted to please us and be our guide.

We were shown the little museum with some
splendid old service books, those huge folios which,
before the present cheap reproduction of modern
small volumes, stood in grand state in the centre
of the choir, and all placed themselves around and
sang from the noble and precious pages.   There
were relics, too, of the times when the Indians
were in their primitive condition, the childlike
pupils of the patient Franciscans.   It was not
much of a display, but its very meagreness made
it pathetic.

Our lay brother took us into the second enclosure ; that is, within the convent proper, where no women are admitted, except in most special cases, and as a mark of honor to noble ladies. Some of us felt quite elated at the distinction thus given to us as men, but the ladies poohpoohed at our airs, for from the neighboring tower they could look down and see into the whole place, and declared there was nothing specially in it. Well, there was not, but there would be if they were there.

We went also into the well-kept cemetery, where a great crucifix kept solemn watch over the sleeping dust of the departed. It was all beautiful with flowers, a lovely place of peace and rest. One cannot help respecting those missions which are so frequently met in California. They represent an immense amount of patient, humble, and persistent labor.

We all took a great, four-horse vehicle in the afternoon for an excursion to Sycamore Cañon, to which spot, however, we never got, and did not regret it a particle. We stopped at an orange ranch half-way, and there we stayed. We wanted to have an " orange wallow," as I called it, and that we got under the trees of a superb orange orchard, where the ground was lush with grass and a general air of luxurious opulence was on every hand. This verdure results, I understand, from the higher elevation of the place, which catches the " high fog" from the Pacific. The moisture of this vapor condenses on the trees and plants, taking the place of rain, and, to a great extent, of irrigation.

As we were winding our way up the steep ascent, with its ever-increasing view down the valley and over the Pacific, we could not but be elated and inspirited with our surroundings. We were, it may be said, a rather noisy crowd.

In this happy state on we went. As we journeyed, we noticed a woman dressed in blue jeans busy at work in her garden. She seemed too busy to notice us. The ordinary rustic curiosity to see the noisy newcomers was entirely absent. She never once looked our way.

In ten minutes or so we were, in various groups, returning from the farmhouse where we had gotten permission to have all the orange wallow we wanted. Then we again met the lady of the blue jeans; but this time she was looking at us with an amused expression on her face, and when one of our company, yielding to an impulse of gallantry, lifted his hat to her, she pleasantly returned the salute, and called out to us, from the height on which she stood, in a clear, ringing voice, " Won't you come up and see my roses ? Come, and you will find more surprises." Of course, we climbed the hill, and soon found ourselves in a veritable fairyland. We were on a spur of the mountain which spread out in a plateau covered with beautiful turf. Rich trees surrounded it on three sides, while on the other it was open to the sea view, revealing to us the curving beach of Santa Barbara, miles away, with the white breakers dashing upon the shore. The great deep beyond was dim and empurpled with the haze, while all around us was a garden glowing with fruits and flowers of kinds that were rare and beautiful, and for the most part strange to us.

After enjoying all this under the guidance of our hostess, who bestowed La France roses and American Beauties among us with liberal hands, we were invited into her house. This was a rambling, one-story structure, beautifully planned, and filled with treasures of art from many climes. The lady of the place gradually let us know in the most simple way that she had travelled far and wide. She was at home in India, and had passed through the principal countries of the world. We spent a good long time in this charmed spot. We were offered refreshment, and left with a sense of gracious hospitality offered in a most graceful way. Her blue jean working dress, for she lived almost at work in her garden, became her well. The only consciousness she showed that she might have wished it otherwise was as she prepared to escort us to our brake; she discarded her sunbonnet and donned coquettishly a little white one of muslin, which, there was no denial, became her better than that she wore at her lovely work.

We waved her farewell as we descended from "Samarcand," the name of her beautiful place, the site of which she herself had selected, planning also her home and all its beauties of tree and flower and fruit.

The poet of the party put his impressions of the whole affair in verse, and here it is:

SAMARCAND

Santa Barbara

How can we speak the glad surprise
   Which met us on that morning ride—
The glory of the boundless skies,
   The mountains in their stately pride !

And greater yet the misty deep,
   Which, huge and vast, swept out afar
In dreaming beauty, silent sleep,
   Which storm, it seemed, could never mar.

But better than the boughs which hung
   With golden fruit and blossoms sweet,
And better than the flowers which clung,
   Were words which there our hearts did greet.

They said, "Come see my roses red ;"
   They came from frank, sweet face, and eyes
Which gleamed with happy mirth, and said,
   "Come here for further yet surprise."

We climbed the mount, we grasped the hand,
   We looked upon the gracious face ;
We saw the wealth of "Samarcand,"
   The Place, and Lady of the Place.

Fit setting for so warm a heart
   Seemed orange grove and mountain side ;
Of nature's best she seemed a part,
   Yea, more ; of all, its greatest pride.

Too soon the time to part drew near,
   The farewell words at last were said ;
But memory ever will hold dear
   Her Home, Herself, her Roses red.

6

XII

Leaving Santa Barbara.—Delay at Saugus.—Viewing the
    Wreck.—Brentwood.—The Mission Mass.—The Social
    Afternoon.—The Garden and the Homing Pigeons.—
    The Grape-Shot.—The Chinaman's Pipe.

WE had yet one more sweet glimpse of Santa
Barbara as we left in the early morning hour. It
was soon hidden from our view, but not from our
memory, where it will ever abide, a place of sunshine and flowers, where the old and the new
stand face to face—the old ocean and the everlasting hills, and the fresh young life of California,
with its exuberant surroundings and genial hospitality.

Our next point was Brentwood, which we hoped
to reach ere the close of day, but a wreck on the
line ahead kept us for hours waiting at a place
called Saugus until the track could be cleared.

Saugus was as forlorn as a muddy beach at low
tide, but some of us made the most of our unpromising surroundings. The uncertainty of the
moment of our departure kept us ever within

sound of the warning whistle of the engine, so
that our little rambles in the woods adjoining
were rather nervous and fitful, but yet better than
nothing.

After all, it is a comfortable thing to be safe
away from a wreck, and a detention for our secu-
rity from accident ought to bring gratitude rather
than fretfulness at all times.

In due time "All aboard!" was sounded, and
then off we were, climbing up into the mountains.
It was a continual feast to look at their ever-
changing forms, and watch the curves and twists
of the railroad as it scaled their heights.

We reached the wreck, the cause of our delay,
and even in our rapid glimpse of it we could see
the havoc which had been done in that one "smash
up." Sacks of flour were hurled hither and
thither, their contents scattered on the rocks; cans
of fruit were shot about like warlike projectiles;
and the eccentric heaping of engine, tender, and
freight cars gave us an idea of the impetus of the
force which caused the whole disaster. Fortunately no lives were lost.

It was Sunday morning when we reached Brentwood. It was a scattering village of detached
houses in the midst of a vast plain through which
the railroad ran, straight as an arrow, from horizon

to horizon. The somnolence of Sunday and of nature hung over all, giving little promise for the twenty-four hours we were to stay there; yet unpromising as it all seemed, we passed there a very enjoyable time.

We were left to our own devices all day, for Dr. and Mrs. Humphreys and the members of his family, went off in the early morning, to visit some relatives ranching in the foot-hills of the encircling mountains, which enclose the vast plain, on which Brentwood stands. How beautiful and ever-varying those mountains were! They told us new stories from morning until night—now a romance of purple and gold; again, a story of less heroic character, as they stood out plain and clear in the sunshine; and again, a tale of deeper mystery, as the night shadows gathered upon their sides, and the moonbeams gave a strange brilliancy to their higher peaks.

Brentwood and all its belongings was before us for the Sunday. After an exploring tour, we found two churches, a Campbellite and a Methodist. They did not look particularly inviting, although the hymn singing in one by the Sunday-school children touched us. We still strolled on and came upon a group of people busily engaged taking flowers into a long, blackened shed which we were told was the town hall, and that there a Dominican monk was to hold services that morning. A fine-looking young German of the tall, black type was busy arranging the rude temporary altar, and a number of ladies and others were assisting him. My German friend offered us an introduction to Father Burke, the monk in question, but we declined, not wishing to intrude upon him before his Mass.

The hour for service came, and we were on hand, with a varied crowd from the town and country adjacent, quite a goodly number. There was a large, white curtain hung back of the altar as a sort of reredos. It did not reach the floor, however, and as the platform was rather high, we had a preliminary view from almost the knees down of all the necessary preparation and vesting, more interesting than edifying. But the service itself,—in the character of the congregation, the mothers with their babies, the young, restless lads, the old people of other days and other climes, and the young people of California growth,—all made up a most interesting study. The music was quite good, being provided by some visitors from San Francisco; two ladies, whom we afterward met, having voices of excellent tone and real culture. An *Ave Maria* and the *Sanctus* were especially

well sung. Father Burke gave an offhand sermon, well arranged and thoughtful, suitable for
Christians of any orthodoxy whatever. It was
good to hear him.

My German friend, after service, again invited
me to call. It turned out he was the tavern-
keeper in the place; so after our pleasant midday
dinner on the " Lucania," we all adjourned to the
hotel, where in the parlor were the choir of the
morning service, several other ladies and gentle-
men, and, taking his ease and enjoyment, also
Father Burke. We spent more than two hours
in the happiest way. Stories were told and songs
were sung, and libations of the best California
vintage were offered us, all ending with " The
Star Spangled Banner," sung by all standing. I
say all standing, for two ladies, said to be Spanish
sympathizers, remained seated glumly on a sofa,
but were good-naturedly drawn to their feet by a
laughing companion, and made to assume the
virtue of patriotism if they had it not.

By this time the train was due, and Father
Burke, the lady singers from San Francisco, and
their friends had to leave us, obedient to the im-
perial mandate, " All aboard!"

My German friend again came to our assistance
in the way of amusements, and invited us into his

hotel garden.   It was a humble little enclosure, but in the centre, coming up through some rock-work, there was an iron jet which he let on, and made a fountain of for our pleasure, quite refreshing to look at.   The distant mountains, too, which appeared so far away as one looked from the open plain, seemed here strangely near and picturesque, when seen through the arched openings of the enclosing trees.   Our friend also had a surprise for us in some homing pigeons of rare excellence, of which he was specially proud.   He showed us his pet prize winner with its eyes and carriage like a genius.   He went in among them, and seemed so tender with them, and interested in them, that it was all a thing of poetry of the highest kind; the great tall man and the fairylike shapes and motions of his beloved birds.   He took out of the cote the very best of the lot, and gave it to one of our young ladies to let fly outside, so that we could see it circle round and round, and then make for its home again.

By this time it was toward evening, and we could descry in the dim distance the return of Dr. Humphreys and his family, as their carriages wound along the plain back again to Brentwood.

Night brought us a silver moon, which added new beauty to all our great surroundings of plain and mountain, and we could look back over a day filled to overflowing with interest and pleasantness, the half of which is not told; but we must at least mention the grape-shot which was picked up on the railroad track, and which set us thinking of how it got there. Was it fired from a Spanish cannon in early days, or by settlers in some Indian difficulty, or marauding trouble, or when?

We must also tell of the happy Chinese laundryman whom we interviewed under the light of the moon, the very picture of placid, contented comfort, as he smoked a huge pipe with stem two feet long. Poor soul, all in his loneliness, coming out from his little hole for a breath of fresh air and a touch of that great nature which is ever so good to us all if we will but let it. Our Chinaman told us that his pipestem was especially valuable, that it had the excellent quality of making the smoke cool, and that such stems, being made of the tea shrub, were very rare. One of our number next morning wished to purchase the said pipestem from " John," but he refused all offers, saying he would not give it for fifty dollars.

XIII

IN San Francisco we had a couple of full days
and fragments of two others, all too short to fully
take in the wonders of that romantic city, so
bizarre, so strange, and in its way so attractive.

After coming across the Bay from Oakland, we
found ourselves in the midst of the noise and
bustle of the railroad yards, fronting on a street
crowded with teams and wagons from morning
until night; and in the night, the ever-resounding
snorts of the iron horse were not found as sooth-
ing as the nightingales of San Remo; but one cannot have everything. If you travel thousands of
miles in the same car, and are proud to reach
home in the same palatial manner, the nuisances

of the depot are of minor importance, after all.

The huge wagons hung low near the ground, groaning under merchandise in transit, and the splendid horses which drew them were worth looking at. The ever-wakeful life of railroad men and their unceasing labors must increase one's respect for that class of people, so strong, so active, so intelligent, and so self-reliant, which garrison the fortresses and outposts of trade all over the American continent. Such a life is a training-ground for possible armies of another kind, which a touch on the American flag, or on our national honor, could transform in a flash into a formidable and reliable force in any emergency.

In my musings while in this busy place, my attention was called to a flagman just opposite where our car was anchored. I explored his shanty and had a good chat with him. His little place was bright without and within. Outside were flowers and shrubs; within not a speck of dust was to be seen. It was as shipshape as the best kind of a New England home, having a place for everything, and everything in its place.

In the intervals of his labor, he had time for a quiet rest on an improvised seat outside his cabin door. That seat attracted me. It was like stone,

but its peculiar shape told me it was a joint from
the vertebræ of a whale. It was just a piece of
gigantic bric-à-brac, well seasoned, which one
might covet. I asked him what he would take
for it. "Oh," said he, "I could not sell that; it
was here before I came, and will remain after me."
One could not but respect the sentiment which
would regard a tradition rather than pocket a
possible dollar. I had too much admiration for
such fine feelings to offer to tempt the man again
with a new proposal.

A little later on in our stay, we all adjourned to
the Palace Hotel, an enormous hostelry which
was once the wonder of the continent, and yet has,
with its huge interior glass court, a certain air
about it quite magnificent.

From there we made excursions to some of the
stock sights of the place. We went out to the
Seal Rocks and saw the Pacific breakers dash up
on the huge crags, where the seals, or sea-lions
rather, for they are not true seals, mowed and
roared and tumbled over each other in their
awkward progress on the cliffs. We saw them
also in their element, darting gracefully through
the waves. We saw Sutro's Baths near by, a
huge structure with splendid accommodation for
bathers. We saw also the grounds and residence

of Sutro, the rich man who built those baths at his own expense, and for the benefit of the people. The grounds of the residence were filled with statues and ornamental sculptures, too lavish for good taste; but, let us admit, at least, that the intention to thus decorate was certainly good. We also saw the Presidio, or army station, and were severely, but most politely, warned off from certain points by armed and mounted sentries. It was a little touch of the war spirit and order, not displeasing. The sentry with whom we parleyed was a type of the American soldier, self-reliant, unconventional, intelligent, and polite. When one looks at such men, they see the new ideas which have discarded forever the millinery of military life. There are no more restraining straps and buckles; no more pipeclay; no more propping up, like trussed fowls, of chest and shoulders; but all is free, natural, and unrestrained.

We drove out over the bare sand hills, which myriads of lupins of various shades of purple and yellow, were doing their best to clothe and glorify. We came to Golden Gate Park in our drive, and thoroughly enjoyed its extent, the glory of its trees and strange shrubs, and, among other sculptures, the splendid monument to Francis Key, the author of the " Star Spangled Banner." From

the park, we could see the surrounding mountains, and on their slopes the distant buildings of
various educational institutions, of splendid proportions.

The great stone cross, commemorative of the
first religious services held on the Pacific Coast
in the time of Sir Francis Drake, loomed up
grandly at some distance from us, but we could
not get our Jehu to drive us to it; there was always
some excuse at hand.   The late George William
Childs, of Philadelphia, caused its erection, to
commemorate these first services of the Church
of England; but a cunning myth is circulated in
San Francisco that it is an advertisement for a
stone quarry !

San Francisco, situated as it is, on a series of
precipitous hills, presents some magnificent and
picturesque views.   It is a sort of gigantic and
altogether exaggerated Edinburgh.   When one
thinks of Edinburgh, however, with its castled
crag and Holyrood, and the gardens right through
the city, one is almost ashamed to compare a bijou
like it, with a huge creature like San Francisco,
which suggests, somehow, a kind of prehistoric
being, of dragon-like shape and unimagined power.

This prehistoric suggestion which San Francisco
gives, is further carried out by the untempered

breath of its climate. The trade winds blow in fiercely in the afternoons, and the chill sea fog creeps over everything with a ferocious persistency quite appalling. The promontory on which the city stands is open to all gales, and one's clothing, throughout the year, must be of such a kind, as always to be capable of resisting borean blasts.

This strange, unfamiliar look of San Francisco, is further carried out by the huge, reddish-yellow bars which mark its form. These are the streets, which ride up and down in uncompromising straight lines and parallels, right over every obstacle which they meet.

The barbaric forcefulness which laid out straight streets sheer over little mountains, has developed in San Francisco the cable-car system, which here reigns supreme, tugging everything along with it.

It is no easy matter for a tenderfoot from the East, to ride in such cars on a first attempt, with either comfort or dignity. On one stretch you are ascending at a fearful angle, then for a brief space you are on the level, only to be whirled up or down, as the case may be, in a few minutes more. When one is sitting sideways, as is usual in street cars, it requires a certain diffused consciousness to preserve one's equilibrium, which, those accustomed to the use of seats always on

the level, cannot readily attain. This self-adjust-
ment once reached, however, and the pivot of per-
manence properly adjusted, one can proudly keep
one's position like a native, and not flop over one's
neighbors at every change of angle, as one must
do, to one's utter confusion, on a first ride in a
San Francisco cable-car on a steep incline.

There were many attractions for me in San Francisco, among friends whom I had known in days
long gone by, in Chicago, Milwaukee, and Racine;
but in our short stay little more could be had than
a handshake, a good-by, and an *au revoir*, which
one hoped, that even the three or four thousand
miles soon to intervene, would not render utterly
impossible.

Of course we saw Chinatown. We emerged
from the Palace Hotel well on in the night, and did
not return until almost a naughty hour in the
morning; but we all felt well repaid for our trip. I
think, though, really, the best part of it was the
feeling of possible danger in the sights before us;
and the spooky appearance of the dark, narrow
streets, into which the moonbeams dropped, revealing to our excited gaze, gliding or stationary
and wretched-looking Chinese, on every hand.
Our guide was a strange specimen, a short, thick-
set man with a queer Pennsylvania Dutch dialect,

and an Irish name, like Duffy or McCarthy, I forget which.   It was droll beyond measure, to hear his description of the joss-house given in a sing-song, full of ludicrous blunders and clipped words. But despite of the comic in our guide, the joss-house itself was solemn enough, and provocative of thought.   It was strange to see altar before altar, all covered with vases and lamps alight, and all manner of bronze bowls and incense burners. It was all so weirdly like what one sees in many Christian churches, and yet with a difference, for the dragons and monster forms were so strangely gruesome and grotesque, that it gave one almost an uncomfortable feeling.   What did it all mean ? Were we at times unconsciously heathen in our cults, or are they at times unconsciously Christian ?   The whole difficulty was summed up in one monosyllable, which escaped from a brother clergyman's lips standing near me, and that one word was an astonished and emphatic " Well!!! "

We are soon aroused from our reverie by the strident tones of our guide, who, taking his stand near a large stove in one corner, exclaims : " Now, ladies and gemmen, y' would s'pose that dis yere stove was for heating this buildin', but it ain't no such thing.   'Tis for sending things to dead Chinamen.   They puts 'em on papers and burns 'em

here, and then they thinks they have 'em.''
Again he would show us the accumulated ashes
in the incense bowls, and tell us that it was kept
to put under the bodies of the '' dead corpses;''
and so on, and so on, until you scarcely knew
whether he himself knew or not what he was talk-
ing about. During all this harangue, a pale-faced
celestial was seated behind a sort of counter in
one corner, with a countenance bereft of all expression, except the suspicion thereon of a high-
bred scorn for us all, as a gaping crowd being led
about among things of which none of us knew anything. This custodian, or priest, whatever he might
have been, had a kind of jaunty cap on his head,
and was comfortably smoking, in the most earthly
manner, a well-flavored cigarette. We bought from
him some joss-sticks as a peace offering, at double
prices, and in a grand manner he bowed us out.

I had asked the guide to draw it mild in his ex-
hibitions, and to omit all places, so to speak, off
color. This he did. We saw a few restaurants,
and a Chinese drug store, where we purchased
some strange medicines which looked more *outre*
and picturesque in their material, than in any
promise of possible effectiveness in their use.
Among these was a dried toad neatly spread out
upon wooden splints. This, we were assured, if

7

boiled into a soup, was an infallible remedy for leanness. Soup we knew was said to be fattening, but he who would drink such a concoction as this dried skin would promise, must be deeply enamored of obesity.

We also saw an opium den. This was horrible enough; but the smoker on exhibition was not so horrible to me as the still, silent figures, stowed away on bunks, in the loathsome darkness of the place. The " John," who was conveniently placed in a lighted place near the entrance, lay prone on the hard boards of his cubicle, bent flat on his side like the letter w, clutching his long, villanous-looking pipe in his hands. Near him was a cat, which we were assured also had contracted " the habit; " not that it too hit the pipe, but that it rejoiced in the heavy atmosphere. The impassive smoker, however, burst into a fit of most intense and humorous laughter, when one of us made an attempt to pronounce some Chinese phrase which he was repeating for us. " Now," said our guide, " he is going to take the long draw." By this time the bit of opium was cooked sufficiently at the cocoanut-oil lamp, and with cheeks distended and eyes closed he sucked in the smoke, and exhaled it in a few moments in a large cloud. I had a lighted cigar in my own hands, and I could not but think that two kindred vices here confronted each other face to face, and my conscience was a bit disturbed; but at once reassurance came to me in a sweet female voice, for one of our ladies said, " Oh, do smoke your cigar; the odor of it is so refreshing in this dreadful place." All over the bunks and floor were crawling black insects, large and small. The guide seeing me shrinking from them said, " Never mind them, they never leave here." By this time we were glad to depart and get into the purer air of the moonlit night.

We walked back to our hotel, passing by balconies lit with Chinese lanterns, restaurants aglow with lights, and numerous Chinese club houses where the celestials, by coöperation, evade certain prohibitory enactments, and in the privacy of their associations, enjoy all their celestial delights.

We also visited a manufacturing jeweller's shop where a lot of goldsmiths were at work. The whole place had on it the mark of utter simplicity. The instruments of the craft were primitive, almost rude, in appearance. Each man was seated before his portion of the work bench, or at a small table, in the narrowest possible space. An open dish containing some nut oil, and a bunch of vegetable fibre for wick, aflame at one end in a tiny light, this, a blowpipe, a few little files, and some lumps of wax was all; but behind this was a patient yellow man, capable of quick motion, but never of ignoble hurry, to whom the present moment was an eternity of time and opportunity, of which he felt that himself, and all his work, were essential parts. But, to our infinite amusement, behind all this was a busy little Chinese woman, who flitted from man to man and bench to bench, criticising, blaming, encouraging, and urging on everybody, with a tongue that never ceased, and eyes and motions as alert and rapid as a humming-bird. Her bright little eyes, her unceasing movement, her evident control of all, was absolutely exhilarating. Woman rules everywhere, or could, if she only would.

I must not omit the mention of a glorious trip out across the harbor, to a watering place full of villa residences, nestled at the water's edge, close under the towering mountains which encompass the whole great expanse. The coloring of the place, the forms of the mountains, and the tints upon the water, all suggest the Mediterranean and other foreign shores.

In the fragments of the days left us in San Francisco, most agreeable hours were spent in stores where Chinese and Japanese goods, in great profusion and splendid taste, were freely open to our view.

An agreeable treat was also given me in a visit to the Bohemian Club, where, through an introduction from a New York friend, I met some delightful and hospitable men. In the club were some capital pictures produced by California artists; among them, a great small painting of the redwoods seen at night, with a camp-fire in the foreground, most Rembrandt-like in effect. Another was full of sunshine and life. It was a group of boys undressing in the blue shade between two yellow sand dunes by the sea; while out in the ocean surf beyond, in the full light, were two or three, already in, having the full frolic of their free pleasure in the blue waters of the Pacific.

But we had yet to see other places, and soon San Francisco was left behind.

XIV

Departure for San José.—Palo Alto.—Advertiser.—Leland Stanford, Jr., University.

OUR next point after leaving San Francisco was San José. On our flight thither, we stopped off for some four hours at Palo Alto, and took a lovely ride through the gorgeous Leland Stanford estate, and also some others; taking in besides, the wonderful Leland Stanford, Jr., University. It was all, it is true, but a glimpse, but a glorious one. Are not our best impressions often but the result of supreme moments! We see and feel in such moments, with an intenseness, which gives us our best conceptions and our most cherished memories. If we approach a scene with the imagination all wrought up, we are often apt to be disappointed; for, there is that in the ideal of all minds which never can be realized. But, as if to make up for this condition of our being, nature and art, each alike, sometimes come upon us unawares, with such unexpected beauty, that our

ideal is accomplished for us, and even more than
realized, before we know it. Then we submit ourselves to our surprise, and are satisfied.

Somewhat in this mood Palo Alto broke upon
us. There were the rich lands in high cultivation,
the spreading trees of various kinds, the vine-
yards, the olive yards, the orchards, the spacious
houses, the glowing gardens all abloom. The
whole was a rich combination gratifying every
sense.

We saw in one of the gardens a beautiful piece
of Greek art brought from Pompeii, a portion of
a graceful curved peristyle of marble, once white
and glistening, but now a rich fawn color, the result of time stretching back to the beginning of
the Christian era or beyond. Every line of the
fluting on the columns, and the carving on archi-
trave and capital, was fresh as if of yesterday. It
stood there like a dream of the far past, made
visible to us here to-day, in a garden of roses in
this enchanting West.

Another object also interested us. It was a
superb living thing which might have served as a
model for the sculptor of the Parthenon frieze.
It was the great blooded horse " Advertiser," for
which some fabulous sum had been offered and refused. I forget who owned the creature, or what

the sum was which was thus offered.   It matters
not.   I remember only the graceful stallion led
out from his stall for us to look at him.   His
glossy coat, his perfect form, his noble attitude,
his fiery eye, his strange look of intelligence—all
these spoke of the art of Athens and the Greeks.
The life and force, which could carve such a creature in marble, seemed to have place also in the
superb living creature himself.   I was struck particularly by his noble bearing, by the contour of
his head, and also by a peculiar length of the
upper lip, having a kind of quivering, prehensile
property, not often seen in such animals.   When
he was led back into his stall, it seemed to me, that
we sightseers, should have apologized to him for
our intrusion.

   We also saw in our short stay the famous Leland
Stanford, Jr., University.   The first sight of the
structure is rather disappointing.   Its low elevation on the broad plain on which it stands, and a
huge chimney for heating and engine purposes
rising above it, give the whole place the aspect of
a machine shop or railroad works; but on closer
approach this impression vanishes.   Then the
spirit of the architect is understood.   He had ample space for his design, and so he laid out a vast,
cloistered parallelogram of one story in height, all

built of a warm-tinted yellowish stone, giving the richest shadows of blue and purple.

It was a delight to gaze down the perspective of these enclosing aisles, and then from the arches to look out on the fountains playing in the sunshine, to see the richness of flowers and trees and shrubs, all overarched by a sky of blue without a fleck of cloud.

How different it all seemed to the quads of Oxford, or the backs of Cambridge, where the yew, the beech, and the ivy give a sombre tone of the past, with which the weather-worn buildings and the clouded skies well accord; while the ever-verdant turf under foot, gives all a touch of a constant life that is ever new.

Here all was different. The court was asphalted, the flowers were as if in baskets, the trees were the product of untiring care. It was all the result of energy and art conquering nature and chaining it down to a definite work.

The whole University speaks of this forceful energy. It is the result of fortune amassed by untiring purpose and sleepless activity; but all the intense activity which it symbolizes has on it the touch of a tragedy, which lifts itself and its conception, into a far higher sphere than ordinary things.

It is the crystallization of affections which shine out from grieved hearts. It is the memorial of an only son taken from boundless fortune and all that earth could promise—taken in the first flush of his beautiful manhood, from parents, whose whole life was centred in his being.

There is a touching pathos in the picture of this youth, as it looks down from the walls of the library, on the group of young students, men and women, gathered there to reap the benefit of the institution which his fortune sustains, and ever will sustain. He was the sole heir to vast estates, to many commercial interests, to great enterprises. All that was his, is now devoted to the uses of those who teach and are taught, in the Leland Stanford, Jr., University.

One leaves the place with regret. One turns back longingly to take a last look at its quaint Spanish architecture, and one treasures up the memories of it all with greatest pleasure. One remembers the quiet of the marble mausoleum in the woods, where father and son rest side by side, waiting for the completion of the family group beyond the tomb. One also calls to mind the beautiful museum which our time would only allow us to glance at; and also, the many pictu-resque homes springing up all about the University, the whole leaving an impression upon us which cannot soon be forgotten.

Our four hours in the luxuriant surroundings of Palo Alto and the University, every moment filled in with busy sightseeing, caused us to enjoy the rest of our further railroad ride to San José.

XV

AFTER leaving Palo Alto, our journey revealed
to us an ideal Californian landscape. We passed
through the lovely Santa Clara Valley. Rich cultivation met our eye on every side, interspersed
with fine forest trees, all hemmed in by the ranges
of the surrounding mountains. These vast masses
enclosed the whole view with their ever-varying
outlines, soft and purple in the distance, while the
foreground of orchards, with their rich herbage, was
all of the deepest green. It was a picture to take
away with one as, indeed, that of a happy valley.
But in this connection the word valley must not
be construed in any limited sense. It was a vast
champaign of almost boundless extent, which the
fairy-like coloring of the mountains, softened by

their great distance, enclosed, as it were, with banks of unmoving clouds. Through this delightful country we sped on rapidly, until at the evening hour, we reached San José, and once more, came to our night anchorage in the station.

We had had a full day of it, and, as if by mutual consent, we separated into various groups to wander at will through the strange streets of the pretty place. It was pleasant to look at the rose-covered cottages and the well-kept lawns, seen by the glitter of the electric light; as also it was pleasant to stroll through the busy streets with the shops all aglow, and the people lounging about in happy leisure.

I wandered off, all alone, to hunt up some friends who had moved to San José from distant Illinois, years and years ago. I found the street and number in a drug-store directory, and strolled on and on under the deep shadows of the overarching trees, losing myself once or twice, but after some inquiry, I was soon piloted to the place and rang the bell. There is always a little trepidation in such an adventure. Will one be remembered? Will the friends be much changed? Will one be welcome? But soon all doubts vanished when my good friend, Mrs. G——, stood in the doorway, lamp in hand. Yes, she was changed; but

the years had made her look more and more like
her dear mother, whose face I could never forget.
Instantly my name was spoken and I was at home.
The whole house was rather topsy-turvy; carpets
all up, and everything in that state of desolation
which house cleaning involves. But what did
that matter? We had a long and good talk over
all the past. I was told how, when they came to
San José in the early days, they had first to go to
New York, then take a steamer to the Isthmus,
to cross that, and then once more embark on the
Pacific for San Francisco, and from thence come
here by team. I was shown the pictures of the
five lovely girls and the boy, a man grown—all
Californians—and I saw that happiness and pros-
perity, which rejoiced me much, had come to
these my friends.

The evening hours lengthened out while our
chat went on, until I had to retrace my steps once
more under the overarching trees to the " Lucania," after promising that I should dine with
the family on the coming Sunday. This I did,
and saw them all, and enjoyed the hour to the
fullest. The Chinese man-servant, cook and but-
ler in one, was noiseless perfection in his attendance, and the works of his art which he placed
before us, were well worthy of our attention; while

California claret, of tenderest texture, helped to whet our appetites and loosen our tongues.

But we must return to the Saturday which intervened before that dinner. The morning was spent in a drive through the town—through the garden would better describe it, for it was all a garden, with rose-embowered roofs or stately mansions framed in by towering palms and stately growths of other graceful trees. It is strange to see the effect which this semi-tropical climate produces on familiar plants. The sweet geranium towers up until it becomes almost a tree, covering the whole ends of houses with its perfumed leaves, and the English lavender emerges from its island modesty, and stands up on this American soil with all the self-assertion of an independent shrub. In one of the parks we saw the little English daisy, but that was the same " wee crimson-tipped flower" that it ever was. It brought tears to the eyes of some of our party, as the springs of home memories welled up within the breast. What volumes do blossoms ever speak to us! A bunch of red primroses, discovered once by chance among the myriad common yellow blooms which gladdened the woods all about us, stands out forever in our memory, as a sudden revelation of beauty— and all for us who found it—which no subsequent possession of far greater worth, has ever yet excelled.

But the friends, the flowers, the fruits, and the foliage of San José, charming as they all were, could not detain us. We were bound for the stars; and at noon or thereabouts, a happy party of us took passage in a large brake, with four horses, for the Lick Observatory on Mount Hamilton. We were armed with an introduction to Professor Schaeberle, the astronomer in charge, and the electric wire had flashed also our coming, beforehand.

It was a merry party that rattled out of San José and looked down on the orchards on either hand as we whirled by. Our ascent was gradual at first, but soon the magnificent, winding roadway, which cost Santa Clara County nearly $100,000 to construct, took us up, and up, ever extending our view, and giving us fresh vistas of surprise, as we dashed by curves and grades which made the nervous among us more nervous still. But there was little to fear with such good drivers and well-trained animals. They knew their business, and were as careful of themselves as if we were not in existence. The ever-increasing panorama of the mountains was full of interest. The great, swelling foothills were yielding and soft-looking in their brown outline, dotted over by huge, woolly-looking, dark green live-oaks and other trees. The whole effect was like a gigantic piece of old Flemish tapestry. If some giant horsemen with winding horns and bounding dogs of like vast scale, and a stag with antlers touching the mountain-tops, and a castle like Walhalla were in our vision, the thing would have been the ancient tapestry, indeed, in true Californian proportions. It was all beautiful as it was, the mossy brown of the mountains, and the dark green of the trees, and over all a cloudless sky, and in our lungs the clear, pure air, full of elation and vigorous life.

Of course in such a mountain drive we changed horses frequently, and at Smith Creek we made a long halt for supper. It seemed that that much-desired meal would never arrive, and the fear that we would miss the sunset view from the summit, added to our impatience. It so happened that there was a rush of visitors that day, and we had to wait our turn while the limited domestic force in this isolated spot, renewed their labors in cooking and serving another meal.

The perfect imperturbability of our host was a thing to admire. No amount of muttered discontent moved him a particle. He did not show impatience even, when we lined up at the dining-room door; by this action, and the rush which it intimated, suggesting that we felt he might come some game upon us, and let some more favored ones in first. When we did make the rush, and saw the well-filled tables, and saw also the patient wife and daughter, neither of them over-robust, who had to do all the work, no " help " wishing to stay up there, we almost felt ashamed of ourselves for our grumbling.

We soon got through our eating, and once more were *en route* for the summit. We got there before sunset all right, and were received in most hospitable fashion by Professor Schaeberle, who showed us through the long halls and into the library, where transparencies and photographs of eclipses and double stars, and various other celestial phenomena charmed us, until at last it was announced that the royal presence of the sun was about to sink to its rest, in the distant west. Then all were soon out on the grand terrace, and as we watched the great, round orb vanish from our sight, a silence fell upon us all, the cause of which it would be hard to put into words. We had seen the great mystery of life move on a point. We thought, perhaps, of the angel trumpeter, who some day will say so that all will hear,

" Time shall be no more ! " We thought, perhaps, of that day when we should close our eyes upon the earthly sun forever, and days for us should be at an end.

As the darkness settled down, so solemnly and grandly on the mountains, we retraced our steps to the Observatory, and followed our kind guide through its many mysteries.

We first looked through some of the smaller telescopes. In one of these, while the glow was still in the heavens, we saw Venus, the evening star, in all its beauty. The earth currents, through which we had to look, gave the glowing planet a purplish tinge and a sort of vibratory motion, which quite suggested the floating movements of the goddess, as she figures in Virgil's verse.

We saw all sorts of instruments, of the most delicate and yet simple character, for recording seismic disturbances of any kind, or, as we might call them in plainer speech, earthquakes. It is most interesting to note how a glass disk, a little lamp-black, a spring or two, a bit of clockwork, and a tracing-pen, will do the work automatically, and record the direction, the duration, and the time of any seismic disturbance at any hour of day or night. The brain which contrived all this cunning machinery, can go to rest and take its needed

sleep, but the wires and traps set to catch the
shakes of the old globe, are always wide awake,
animated ever by the intelligence of the brain
which sleeps, and can sleep in peace; for, when the
brain wakes, it will find that the machine has faith-
fully recorded every quiver of this old, trembling
world.   Professor Schaeberle told me, with quiet
humor, that earthquakes of some kind were always
going on, but so slight that machinery alone could
detect them.

After seeing the many minor attractions of
transit instruments and meridians and other affairs,
which some of us wondered at, in complete, but
polite and interested ignorance, we were at last
ushered into the presence of the great Lick telescope.   The immense dim space in which we stood,
the half-seen figures of the visitors, the professor
and his attendants, with lanterns in their hands,
accenting the gloom by the very light itself, made
up a weird picture.   Then, towering over all, was
the movable dome, with the great notch from top
to bottom of its curved surface, open to the sky,
for the great telescope to reach through; while the
great instrument itself, in its huge proportions, its
intricate machinery, and the wonderful ease of its
movements, as it yielded to the slightest touch of
a hand, seemed like some living thing, some being

of superior intelligence from some other sphere, captive and at work for our pleasure and our profit.   Who can ever forget the mystery of it all in the silent darkness of that night !

But before looking through the great tube, the professor, with quite unintended, but most dramatic effect, called our attention to a black-looking object at the base of the great pier, on which the telescope stands.   It was like an altar, as we saw it in the dimness, but a lantern flash upon the front showed us it was a monument above the last resting-place of James Lick, by whose munificent bequest of seven hundred thousand dollars, the Observatory on Mount Hamilton, with all its wonderful instruments, has been established for all time.

It was a thrilling thing to see there in the dimness that plain, unpretending tomb, and to read thereon the short and simple record:

JAMES LICK.

1796 — 1876.

But what a life story is revealed by the dash which separates those figures, 1796–1876! Eighty years of toil and endurance, toil in early youth, toil in manhood, toil in the midst of amassed wealth, until the inevitable end at last came. He was born in Fredericksburg, Pa., where he received a common school education. He learned the trade of an organ builder and piano maker in Hanover, Pa. He went into business in Baltimore, Md., and also in Philadelphia; but his destiny drove him away to Buenos Ayres, to Valparaiso, and other places in South America, until, in 1847, he settled in California, where he became interested in real estate, and in due time amassed a large fortune. His strong face, which greets one in bronze, at the Mount Hamilton Observatory, bespeaks a powerful and stern character. He never married. He was deemed by those who knew him to be " unlovable, eccentric, solitary, selfish, and avaricious," but when this is said, the memory of it is somewhat condoned, for there was a romance in the case—he was crossed in love.

It is hard to judge of such a man, and of such circumstances. He certainly has made amends for all his shortcomings, or tried to, if they were as related, by his munificent bequests to charity, and above all to pure science. When one looks at his carpenter's bench, preserved as a relic of his workman's life, and then at his tomb in the still

silence and darkness of the great telescope cham-
ber, and then remembers all that this silent, lonely
man has done, one cannot but believe that he
had in heart, all along, great ideals which none of
those about him, in the vulgar strife of life, ever
imagined. What can be more unlike a narrow,
selfish, unlovable, and avaricious man than his
splendid offering of a fortune to keep eternal
watch upon the stars ?

These thoughts danced through one's brain in
presence of it all. We were grateful to the old
man, whose face, singularly like that of John
Brown of Harper's Ferry fame, seemed to em-
body the tragedies and aspirations of life; and we
thought of his silent dust beneath us, as through
his gifts we looked at Jupiter and his moons, and
noted the strange belts which band the planet,
brought near to us by the lens of the Lick telescope. We saw also the crested edge, glittering
like molten silver, of the moon of this our own
planet, and longed to wait until Saturn should
rise, and other wonders open before us. Professor
Schaeberle made me the fascinating offer to stay
all night, and go down the mountain in the early
morning; but I kept with the party, and, well after
eleven at night, we started on the home run down
the mountain to San José.

The coming up was grand indeed, but the going down was better. The great moon flung its radiance over the vast expanse. It was a symphony in gray and silver. It was a downward plunge into black mysteries of overhanging mountains. It was delirious with possible dangers. It set one's heart throbbing, and the best relief we could have was in song and shout which roused the echoes of the night.

We subsided into silence when we reached safety and the plain, and were rather bored than otherwise, as we cantered into the deserted streets of San José at half-past two o'clock in the morning. How tame seemed the dull surroundings of even that pretty place at such an hour—a few saloons yet aglare, a light in an occasional window, all the rest ghostly, silent, and yet commonplace, too, after our splendid excursion to the stars.

XVI

WE stayed at San José over Sunday, and attended church morning and evening, furnishing
from our number the preacher for both services.
The church had a good choir of men and boys,
surpliced, which was, very sensibly, placed near
the organ in one of the transepts. A much better
arrangement this is than putting all in the com-
pass of a small chancel. To have choristers close
up to the altar is not a commendable use, though
very general. The structural choir of a cathedral
gives ample room for singers and worshippers,
with dignified and clear space about the chancel
proper. The ordinary parish church, in its whole
extent, should be treated as if it were just such a
structural choir, with the singers well among the
people in raised seats, for the prominence of their
office and the better effect of the music.

We had time on Monday to take another stroll among the roses and palm trees of San·José, and then the car "Lucania" in the forenoon took all our party, except one, to Santa Cruz, for an excursion to the Big Trees, about ten miles from there. All this I missed. From the leaves of the diary of one of the party I quote the impression of the trip:

"When we reached Santa Cruz we found a four-horse stage and a carriage awaiting us, into which we got, and were driven back into the woods about ten miles, along a road that wound round with a deep cañon on one side, at the bottom of which ran a river. We finally forded this river, and went into deeper woods, where we found the 'big trees.' They were a grand sight, these solemn old trees, said to be four thousand years old, some of them towering up three hundred feet or so, and sixty and ninety feet in circumference. We all got into one, and our party of thirteen had plenty of room left for several more people. This tree was called after General Frémont, who lived in it while surveying in this region. Before that, it was occupied by a trapper, whose children were born in it. There are sixty acres of these trees which have been preserved from the ruthless greed that is rapidly destroying those priceless giants of the ages."

It was a regret to me that I could not have seen the mystery of those venerable trees, but I had a duty to perform in visiting some relatives residing near Gilroy. It gave me a nearer impression of the Santa Clara Valley and its life. My visit was to a fruit ranch entirely given over to the growth of prunes. The part of the great plain where I was, is cut up into small farms, and these are tended, usually, by the members of the family. The work is limited and light. After the trees are planted, nature, pretty much, does all the rest. When the fruit is ripe is the time of most applied and constant labor. Then, under the shadows of the live-oaks, the whole family attend to the curing of the fruit, which has to be dipped in lye and dried in the open air. It is a pretty and pastoral occupation; and with a horse, and a cow, and some poultry, an easy and comfortable life can be had. It lacks, however, the robust discipline of legitimate farming, with its varied enterprises, and constant changes of crops, of times and seasons. It is a lotos kind of existence, and when I heard of the meeting of reading circles, and of whist clubs, in which regular accounts of rubbers were kept, all through the winter, I knew that leisure was ample and life easy.

While in Gilroy I saw the little Episcopal

church, and enjoyed the happy pride of the old English gentleman, who for more than thirty years, had been senior warden, and had seen Breck and the other California pioneers who labored arduously for the Church in early days. I understood that Breck had planted the two eucalyptus trees which guarded the entrance porch of the little building, trees which have now grown up to be quite large and imposing.

Leaving Gilroy, I awaited our Santa Cruz party at a junction somewhere, and joined them for our run to the Hotel del Monte, and Monterey.

As in all Santa Clara Valley, our way was through fruits, and flowers, and rich vegetation, until at last, we were once more at anchor, in the grounds of the Hotel del Monte.

After tea we wandered out in the twilight through the umbrageous woods, and found that we were separated from the ocean only by a fringe of trees and shrubs, and some sand dunes, over which we had an exciting climb.

The lonely walk, with the roar of the breakers in our ears, and their white foam breaking upon the beach, was a charming close for our day, whether we had seen the solemnity of the giant sequoia, or the humbler conditions of rural life on a ranch.

Stunted cedars in contorted shapes, battered and twisted by storms, began to look more weird in the gathering gloom, but before the light had quite faded out, we had filled our hands with bunches of a pale pink flower, like a morning-glory, with which the sands were dotted. The little fragile flower clung tenaciously to the shifting ground in which it grew, and gathered from all its hopelessness of surroundings, a vigorous life, much of tender beauty, and a fragrance which was refreshing. Nature always shows us how to make the best possible use of any environment whatever. Here, in sands which shifted, amid storms which blew, in utter humility and loneliness, the flower developed firmness, beauty, and fragrance, and gave evidence of constant vigor and of useful life.

We had two full, glorious days at Del Monte, and they were hours of utter enjoyment. The hotel and its well-kept and extensive grounds were enough for a week, at the least, of intense pleasure. The site is a promontory of sand dunes, covered with pine and other native forest trees. The surrounding waters, the yellow sands, the clear, delicious air, the equable climate, the illimitable ocean—these were the raw material for the exquisite result, which one sees at Del Monte.

In the immediate neighborhood of the hotel the landscape gardener has done his best. There, one hundred sixty acres of well-kept grounds feast the eye. Irrigation brings the life-giving current to the sandy soil, and, while we look almost, the turf is green and velvety, the flowers bloom, and the fruits appear.

Nothing can be more bewitching than the winding drives to the hotel. Great forest glades intercept the view, and give impression of still greater distance; or, a vista opens before one, and the huge pines tower up, their naked trunks wreathed closely to their topmost branches, with ivy and other creeping plants.

Wherever one looks there is evidence of intelligent care. One sees it in the rich flower-beds, models of good taste; in the arboretum; in the cactus garden; in the Maze; in the unexpected groups of cultivated plants, where the enclosed garden joins on to the outlying wild. And, in this wild itself, what beauty does one find! The great ocean, the cliffs, the sea-lions, the Chinese shell-gatherers; the winding drive of eighteen miles, by ocean, through rich land, and through the wild-wood, winding back again to the hotel, and all its graceful beauty and luxury. The place has all the sumptuousness of an English ducal

palace standing on its ancestral grounds, with the
added charm here, of space, and vastness, and that
the whole place belongs to every eye which sees it
—that is, if the hand can dip into the pocket and
pay the necessary bills. But even without this, it
does seem to belong to everybody in a certain
true sense. The American hotel of every class,
has about it a generous air of freedom for all,
which is most remarkable.

We were independent of the place in our own
well-appointed car, and yet how freely all was at
our bestowal; the corridors, the music, the reading and reception rooms, and all the magic perfection of the gardens. All was free as air, and
we could wander at will, by the lovely lake, or in
the charming gardens, or in the splendid hotel,
without let or hindrance.

Here is a place where one might enjoy a thor-
ough good rest, lapped in soft airs, close to the
throbbing bosom of mother earth, within sight
and sound of the sea, and housed in a hostelry
which on every side speaks of comfort and refinement. There is no gaud or glitter, but ever the
suggestion of home and all that home means.

On one of our days there we took the eighteen-
mile drive which I have incidentally mentioned
above. It brought us through the old town of

Monterey, a little sleepy place, with many relics yet in it, of the days of '49. Houses still remain, of which the bricks, or iron plates, used in their construction, were brought from Liverpool or Australia, or other points, when upon the shores of Monterey the fierce tide of adventure dashed high, made eager for effort by the thirst for gold.

During our stay at Monterey we—that is, some of us—passed hours on hours strolling on the sands, and reclining in utter abandon on the shore. It was, to the full, the unutterable delight of an entirely irresponsible existence, which took no thought of time, not even of its flight, and luxuriated in the clear, pure air, the dashing breakers at our feet, and the blue heavens above.

There was little of minute attraction upon the beach. It seemed as if all was on too huge a scale for mere minor attractions. There were no rocks to sit upon, but a whale's huge skull, half buried in the sand, made a good enough seat, and débris of that colossal character was all about us.

But it mattered not. The very place itself, and the great Pacific, stretching off westward to the Orient, gave scope enough for the wings of our imagination, and we had present pleasure also, as we lay, in complete idleness, prone upon the warm sands.

The declining sun, however, warned us to retrace our steps once more to the " Lucania,"
where all the pleasures of home awaited us, and
the varied experience of our day gave us conversation until bedtime.

But before that hour, we were on our way back
once more to San José, where, the next day, we
spent some hours renewing our former pleasant
experiences, even with greater zest. Our ladies,
who went out for a walk, came back laden with
gifts of flowers from hospitable friends, the acquaintances of the moment; and, as we started
from San José for Oakland, our car looked like a
bower of roses, laden with perfume.

9

As we turned our backs on San José, we began
to feel that we were heading for home, and were
descending from romance and flowers, to the
more commonplace conditions of existence. I
question if it would be good for us to lead too
long, the ideal and refined Bohemian life, such as
a well-appointed car, and no care, affords.

It was with a sort of shock, that, after hours
of travel, through smiling plain and upland, we
found ourselves in the prosaic environment of
Oakland.

Our car was run out to the end of a pier, which
stretched for miles, it seemed, into the bay.
The vast expanse of water about us, the great
city away off across the bay, and the frail-looking,
but yet perfectly safe, piling on which our car had

place, gave a tone of empty loneliness to everything, and we could not but feel gloomy.

We were becoming fastidious. We wanted "roses, roses all the way," and absolutely were oblivious to the energy which had created this huge pier, crowned with the really splendid ferry-house, and a ferry-house is no uninteresting thing. How little do we think that the whole ferry business in the United States, especially in great centres such as New York, presents the most distinctively American thing we have; the very triumph of common sense and directness of means to the proposed end.

We availed ourselves of the splendid ferry here at Oakland, for a little run once more in San Francisco. My errand was to try and hunt up the Russo-Greek church, and see something of it. I got to the place, and saw the exterior of what was once a magnificent residence, but now a decayed mansion in an unfashionable part of the city. It was given an ecclesiastical effect by being topped with several melon-shaped domes of zinc, brightly painted; these, and the pale blue on walls and doors and windows, gave quite the effect of Russia. My visit, however, was fruitless. The fathers were all out, and a servitor in attendance opened the door, only a few inches, for a cautious parley.

That glimpse showed me some rather rich paintings in the interior of the dwelling, but I had to rush back to our car without waiting for the return of the fathers, or the view of the church, which, I am sure, they would be glad to show me.

Once off from Oakland, we were indeed on the home-stretch, but we had the mountains to climb, and much more to see.

We passed through Sacramento, the capital of the State, merely giving it a glance, as we journeyed on into the glory of the mountains.

But of these mountains, how shall we speak! It was all a grand crescendo of magnificence, until the snowsheds, erected over the tracks, shut out the splendor of the scenery from our view. But even the glimpses through the chinks were worth looking at. We saw far beneath us the silver shield of a lonely and lovely lake, where in spirit we went. We saw, too, the glory of sunset tints upon the frozen peaks of distant heights. We saw, too, the great lines of the mountain-sides, in successive sweeps, pine-clad and lovely, but gigantic in their vast and repeated lines. The whole ride through those sheds was tantalizing and yet interesting. It certainly was a daring thing to conceive a protection from the winter's snow, of such extent; and to keep it all in repair,

ever watched, and tended, must be an enormous
task. It was a splendid sensation to climb those
mountains on our iron horse, but yet one would
fain see them better, and loiter a little among the
camps and mining towns, and know more of the life.

My attention was aroused to the fearful effects
of hydraulic mining as we journeyed on ever
upward. Here and there, one could see the
fearful work which ensued from such methods.
The whole face of a mountain would be torn off
bare, and the valley beneath filled in with refuse,
to the depth of three hundred feet. It all looked
like a great wound on the venerable mountains,
while the river-beds in the valleys were choked,
and distorted from their channels.

A brakeman who was showing me a pocketful
of nuggets and specimens, laughed me to scorn
when I bemoaned the scarred and tortured look
of the hills in sight. "What," said he, "are
mountains good for but to get such stuff as that
out of them?" as he tossed up a fragment of
gold in the air, and caught it on his open and
greedy hand. But, after all, how much more im-
portant mountains are as mountains, than mere
gold-bearing protuberances, and how much more
precious rivers are as life-givers to man and beast,
rather than gold-bearers in their shifting sands.

We were glad to know that legislative enactments have been made upon such mining proces-
ses, and that certain restrictions and limitations
are in force, to protect nature against wasteful
greed, and the reckless spoliation and destruction
of mountain-side and valley stream.

After our climb up the mountain, towards evening we found ourselves at Reno. A wait for supper is made here (we were, of course, independent
of such wayside places), during which we stretched
our legs on the platform, looking at the many
odd-looking people in view.

A freakish notion got into me to be odd also, so,
just to astonish the natives, I donned my Japanese
kimino, made of camel's-hair cloth of light buff
hue, reaching down to my heels. With this on,
I dared one of our ladies to walk with me, offering her my arm. This she did, with a good grace,
and we certainly were the observed, if not the
admired, of all observers.

Some of our party followed us at a little distance to gather up the remarks. "Here comes
Brigham Young, I guess," was one of them; another was, "That's Pope Leo, ain't it?" and yet
another was, "No, it's Bishop Sommers." But
in the midst of the fun, of which of course I
seemed to be oblivious, my eye caught the grave

face of a simon-pure Jap, in American dress, standing by, with eyes, as wide open as he could get them, evidently mystified at my appearance. He could vouch certainly for the genuineness of the kimino, but the *tout ensemble* was too much for him. I felt really sorry for the poor little Japanese, he looked so lonesome, all alone in the crowd. Possibly he might have felt badly that his possible brother countryman did not stop and speak with him!

After leaving Reno, our way took us through Nevada, which we passed in the night. When day dawned upon us we found ourselves in desolate places, more lonely desert than anything we had yet seen. The following poem by Charlotte Perkins Stetson most vividly describes the death-like aspect of the place. It is called—

A NEVADA DESERT

" An aching, blinding, barren, endless plain ;
   Corpse-colored with white mould of alkali,
   Hairy with sage-brush, shiny after rain,
   Burnt with the sky's hot scorn, and still again
    Sullenly burning back against the sky.

" Dull green, dull brown, dull purple, and dull gray,
   The hard earth white with ages of despair,
   Slow-crawling, turbid streams where dead reeds sway,
   Low wall of sombre mountains far away,
    And sickly steam of geysers on the air."

In due time we reached Ogden, a busy-looking place. We did not leave our car, however, for any inspection, waiting for the short run to Salt Lake City, where we were to spend the night and the next day.

In the midst of all the car-tracks, and the many signs of commercial activity, a capering Indian, with a blanket flung round his shoulders, amused us by his childish glee and activity. He was in the exuberance of his wild freedom, among all the business and anxieties which civilization brings. What did he care for it all! He was having a good run, and, for the fun of it, was racing with a young fellow on horseback, and was making rather good time, too. I was interested in this child of the past, this offspring of wild life, as without thought or heed for anything but the present moment, he lived out his day.

In a short time we were at the city of the Mormons, seeing in the distance, as we approached it, the spectral waters of the Great Salt Lake.

XVIII

WE had a full day in Salt Lake City, altogether
too short a time for that interesting place, but we
made the most of it and saw much.

We were favored with letters of introduction to
Governor Wells, whom we found in the State
House, in most democratic fashion. He seemed
a perfect type of Utah, as seen at its best, cheerful and healthy, utterly unconventional. He
seemed kindly by nature, and not from mere rules
of etiquette. He received us in the office of the
secretary of state; and, in his eagerness to ar-
range for some pleasure for us, in our short stay,
he did not even think of asking us to be seated.

An additional carriage was soon hospitably
placed at our disposal, in the kindest manner, and

in it the governor himself gave us his company. We went first to the great Zion Coöperative Store, a huge establishment run by a joint-stock company, all members of the Church of the Latter-Day Saints, or Mormons, as their more familiar designation runs. Here, one could see that mixture of everyday life and religion, which is such a marked feature of the Mormon development.

Mormonism, sprung from American soil, has developed within itself the ideas of Church and State, and the limitations of individual freedom and responsibility, which one would imagine only possible under the most extreme conditions of belief in the divine right of kings, and the more positive divine right of a visible church.

There is nothing new under the sun, and the principles which we supposed America never could brook, are here seen in embryo, or in fact, by the thoughtful observer. In view of the comfort and happiness which one sees in Utah, and the mutual sympathy which the ideas I have mentioned exhibit, one is forced to pause and ask himself, May there not be an object-lesson for us in all this? May we not have thrown away from our social state, with too stern a hand, all reliance upon churchly influence, and exaggerated also that idea

of personal independence, so dear to us, forget-
ting that the individual, in all the relations of his
life, is a part of the state, a member of the body
of the nation, and should be the object of its sympathy, its care, and its government, at all times
and in all places ?

It was my second visit to Salt Lake, a place
which has always interested me because of the
social and religious problems which one sees there.
In my last visit I happened casually to meet a
priest of the Roman Catholic Church, and asked
him offhand what he thought of things around
him.   He looked at me fixedly for a moment, and
then said, " There is not an organization on earth
that can compare to Mormonism, in its wide scope,
its great grasp, and its practical application."

I am inclined to think he is right.   It was my
accidental privilege to be in the city, during my
former visit, while the semi-annual conference of
the Latter-Day Saints of Utah Valley was being
held.

The huge turtle-shell Tabernacle, easily seating
twelve thousand people, was filled daily.   I saw
the rank and file of Mormons, the sturdy agricul-
turists and their wives, the latter like what one
remembers of Primitive Methodists, apparently
utterly oblivious of all personal adornment; they

were, however, crowned with a maternity of which they seemed proud, as they held their children in their arms.

At one end of the great ellipse of that Tabernacle rose up, tier on tier of church officers, grade by grade, the Seventies, the Bishops, the Angels, the Apostles, up to the tripartite headship of three Presidents, the first of which was Elder Woodruff, venerable, simple, and wise in appearance. Back of all was the great organ, and a well-trained choir of three hundred singers.

I heard a number of speeches or sermons, all offhand, and some of them rambling, but the aside excursions were usually on practical matters, or to emphasize the fact that the Latter-Day Saints were the salt of the earth, the power to lead this nation upward from its bloodshed and wrong-doing; and hints were also given, here and there, that God would yet avenge the blood of the prophet slain at Nauvoo.

The most striking speech was that made by Mr. Cannon. He looked like a well-set-up New York business man, faultlessly dressed in an Albert frock coat, with rubicund countenance and flowing mutton-chop whiskers. It was absolutely refreshing to hear him, in his clear-cut sentences, declare that he was then and there speaking under the direct inspiration of the Holy Ghost. The President, Elder Woodruff, at the conclusion of the meeting, gave his sanction to all that was said, thus sealing it as inspired, by his declaration.

A superb anthem by Gounod then floated out over that vast audience, as all remained seated, taking in the power of the music at their ease. At its close Elder Woodruff rose, and all rose with him. With a trembling voice he blessed all in the triune name of God, and the whole assembly scattered in a few moments through the surrounding doors of the Tabernacle.

The Eisteddfod of our Welsh citizens was in full blast in Salt Lake at the same time, and at night I attended the concluding concert. It was an enthusiastic occasion. There were strangers from points quite distant, and the place was packed. The acoustic qualities of the Tabernacle gave wonderful power to both organ and voices, and the effect of the whole was very fine.

While I was scanning the audience and choir with my opera-glass, one of the ushers asked me if he might look through it. Of course he could. But I noticed that he kept pretty steadily to one point in the choir. On remarking that fact to him, he laughed and said, " Yes, I was looking at my best girl; there she is, near the centre, dressed in heliotrope crêpe.'' I .looked, too, and saw a remarkably pretty young woman. He further told me that he was a Mormon, and so was his sweetheart; that they were going to marry, and that they were both opposed to polygamy. He was a bright young fellow, and in our conversation he told me that he had been admitted to some of the higher grades in the Temple, and that there were Mormons of the lower type, who never could get inside its walls.

This leads me to speak of the strange combination of utter, naked simplicity in the ordinary worship of the Mormons, and the extreme of ritual observances which have place in the secrecy of the Temple. In the Tabernacle, when I first saw it, there was not a symbol of any kind visible, no cross, no flower, no sign. In my recent visit, however, in honor, possibly, of the new Statehood of the former Territory, the Star of Utah, draped at each side by the Stars and Stripes, appeared over the organ, and some motto, which I forget, at the other end.

The Mormon Temple is a huge structure of cut granite, brought from the neighboring mountains on canals constructed for the purpose. It is surmounted by six pinnacles of considerable height, and as seen from a distance, has a good effect.

In architecture it is, however, quite nondescript, but doubtless admirably adapted for its purposes. It was thrown open to invited guests among the Gentiles, or non-Mormons, the morning before its consecration, for a few hours' private view.   I have been told that the various rooms and passages were quite gorgeous and impressive in their furnishing and decorations.   Since then all such visitors have been shut out, the only entrance thereto has been kept closed, and will be, as the Mormons say, until the second coming of Christ.

The great building stands in its own grounds, surrounded by flowers and shrubs, kept in beautiful order.   Outsiders can approach to within eight or ten feet of the front door, but no farther.

A small building at one side gives admission to the faithful, who enter therefrom, to the Temple itself, by means of a connecting underground passage.

Mormonism is a most interesting exhibition of Primitive Methodism, of socialism in certain of its aspects, of Judaism, Freemasonry, and ancient Gnostic ideas, all combined with a compact hierarchy, which includes various orders of priests, the whole thing in perfect working order, taking thought for all, in all things, both of soul, mind, body, and estate.

We were certainly charmingly treated by the Mormons we met, and one must have for them respect and admiration. It did me good also to see one of the ladies who were with us, gowned in exquisite taste, quite a contrast to the rank and file of the Tabernacle. Her costume was a symphony in green, carried out in all its details perfectly, even to the gloves, the sunshade, and its malachite handle. We cannot soon forget the hospitality, the grace, and the sweetness which made us at home in Salt Lake City, and asked us to come again.

I think I cannot do better to close this Salt Lake chapter than to quote *in extenso* the very full notes from Mrs. Morgan's diary, which here I do:

" At ten A.M. the carriages came to take us out, and we drove first to the State House, where we found Governor Wells, to whom Dr. Humphreys had an introduction. The governor received us most kindly, and he and Mr. and Mrs. Hammond came driving with us, and pointed out the various objects of interest. We first drove through the business streets, visiting a large department store, and from there to the Mormon Tabernacle, which is a very peculiar building, something like an enormous turtle, the dome roof coming low down and resting on brick buttresses. Between these buttresses are large doors, so that, it is said, this huge building, able to hold twelve thousand people, can be emptied in four minutes.

" Inside, a large gallery runs all round, and we walked to the opposite end, where we distinctly heard a pin dropped at the place from which we started, such are the perfect acoustic properties of the house."

I may here add that a really gruesome effect was also produced by the mere rubbing together of the hands of the gentleman who dropped the pin. The distinct swish-swish of the contacting palms was terribly audible.

Mrs. Morgan proceeds to tell us further:

" The organist kindly played us a couple of selections, and, whether the organ was unusually good, or whether it was the effect of the building, I cannot say, but I never enjoyed music more. We afterwards all joined in singing ' My Country, 'tis of Thee.'

" The Temple is a handsome building in the same enclosure, built of granite, but ' Gentiles ' are not admitted to the inside.

" We then were driven past the different residences of Brigham Young: the Lion House, where three of his widows still reside; the Bee

Hive, and the house · where his favorite wife, Amelia Folsom, a cousin of ex-President Cleveland's wife, resided.   Brigham Young had seventeen wives, and fifty-seven children.   We passed through the Eagle Gate, erected by Brigham Young, seeing also a fine site where he intended to build a college or seat of learning.   We then went to a point where we had a beautiful view of the valley in which the city of Salt Lake lies, and a most remarkable and exquisite view it was.   All around were the grand, snow-capped mountains, guarding and holding, as it were, in the hollow of their hands, the city, with its wide streets, and lines of straight, tall Lombardy poplars, and its thousands of little homes, small and cosy, usually not more than one story in height. Of course there were mansions and houses of more pretentious aspect, but it seemed to me essentially the workingmen's home.

" The statue of Brigham Young adorns the centre of the town, and while one cannot but abhor certain of his religious views, one cannot but acknowledge that he was a far-seeing man of great ability.

" It is stated that, great as has been the growth of the city, it has not reached the limit laid out for it by Brigham Young, when he and his handful of followers first settled in the then arid and desolate plain, with its brooding circle of white-tipped hills.

" We returned to our car for dinner, and afterwards the governor arrived, bringing with him Colonel and Mrs. Clayton. Our car, at the governor's request, was attached to the regular passenger train to Saltair, a point some five miles distant, on Great Salt Lake. We found there a vast pavilion and bathing establishment, capable of accommodating thousands. The water of the lake is so strongly impregnated with salt, that nothing except a sort of minute shrimp lives in it. It was too early in the season for us to take a dip. We were assured that it was impossible to sink in the water.

" On our way back we passed Colonel Clayton's salt beds, into which the water is pumped and left to evaporate. The salt which remains is piled into great heaps. Some of it, in its crude state, is shipped to the silver mines, where it is used in the reducing of silver from the ore. Some of the salt is taken to the refining houses, to be manufactured into the article of domestic use. We spent a pleasant hour in the great pavilion at Saltair, and then returned in the car to the city, where our kind friends took leave of us, Mrs.

Clayton telling me, before going, that I greatly resembled a daughter of Brigham Young's by his first wife! As Mrs. Clayton herself was of the Mormon faith, as was also Governor Wells, I took it, as it was intended to be, as a compliment."

Night was settling down upon us as we turned eastward from Salt Lake City, with faces homeward bound.

The picturesque desert, with its purple hills and terraced mountains, was all concealed by the darkness. At the early morning hour we reached Glenwood Springs, but decided not to stay there, and continued on without delay to Colorado Springs, reaching there on the evening of a day, never to be forgotten, of which we will tell in the next chapter.

XIX

Glenwood Springs. — The Pool. — The Vapor Baths. —
Through the Cañons.—Leadville.—Colorado Products.
—Cañons in New York.

WHEN we reached Glenwood Springs, it was in
the early morning. The place from the railroad
station does not look inviting, and so it was decided to push on to Denver.

This was a loss, for Glenwood Springs has many
advantages, worth seeing, and a hotel of real comfort and elegance. The hot springs there are
quite extensive, and the medicinal baths are delightful. The bathing places are in the highest
style of art, elegantly fitted up with all that
modern appliances, following ancient models, can
accomplish. There is also a huge, open-air swimming-pool, filled with water, from the hot springs,
giving most luxurious enjoyment.

It was my good fortune, on a former visit, to enjoy both it, and the further pleasure of a natural
vapor bath within the rock recesses of one of the

mountains. It was a weird experience. It was late one evening, and I happened to be the only bather there. The negro attendant, a most obliging fellow, took me in charge. Under his directions, after disrobing, he gave me a shower bath of cold water, and then, with a wet towel on my head, he ushered me into a rocky cavern. Some boards extended over fissures in the ground, from whence one could hear the gurgling of the boiling springs far beneath. The rocks overhead leaned against one another, and their great crevices were dark with shadows. There were a few plain wooden benches, blackened with the sulphur fumes; but, as if to assure one that the savage-looking place was really tame, after all, an electric light, in full glare, hung down from above, making the strange surroundings visible in all their mystery of heat beneath, and blackness below and beyond. I watched the experiment of the vapor upon myself, and soon was in a profuse perspiration. My faithful negro cautioned me not to be too long in my first attempt, so I was soon out again to get the protection of another wet towel on my head. After that, all was enjoyment. The whole experience was unique, and in due time I had the further luxury of a good rub down, and a lounge for some time on a couch, helped on also, by a cup of good, black coffee. I could scarcely tell which was best; to float in sulphur water in the open air, with others, under the bright light of day, in the big pool; or, to be utterly alone in the clefts of the everlasting mountains, surrounded by their mysterious warmth, and melted by their embrace. It seemed to me the last ought to have the preference.

As I have said, our party decided to press on from Glenwood. Hours were precious on the homeward run, and to have a whole day for the wonders of the Colorado mountains was something.

We first passed through the cañon of the Grand River, a fitting prelude to all that was to come. Then we travelled along the Eagle River Cañon, and, last of all, experienced the wild wonders of the Royal Gorge. It was a day of continued excitement and exalted pleasure. It is hard to put in words the impressions of these immense rocky passes.

One may think of the giant forces which cleft asunder their rugged sides in times so far removed as to be scarcely conceivable.

Then, as one sees the detached rocks, and the great moraines at the mountain bases, and notes the clinging trees, and wild shrubs, and many flowers, one must think of the rolling seasons, the heat, the frost, the forces of the wind, and the storm, and the constant changes which come with rain and sunshine, with growth, and with decay.

And then, wherever one looks, there, at right hand, or at left of the railway track, is the rushing river, roaring on without stop or stay—day and night—forever. It was these streams which gave a hint of the pathway; first, to the red man, and then to the frontier trapper, and gold-hunter, and last of all, to the engineers who built the iron track over which we were speeding, swiftly, and in peace.

The picturesque effect of all is as varied as the thoughts which must come in such a place. The rapid motion of the train, the ever-changing point of view, as the track winds its sinuous way by the tortuous river-bed—all gives a sort of motion to the vast, overhanging cliffs, which seem to dance past one, like giants on a frolic.

I remember once making the journey through these passes, going west from Denver. The view from the car windows was not enough for me. I planted myself on one of the car platforms, linked my arm round the railing, and with my feet on the steps, sat on the floor, swinging out, as far as I safely could, to take it all in. Thus, oblivious of the dust, I sat for an hour, and at last, satiated by the views on views, returned contented to my seat.   Just then a brakeman said to me, " We are now entering the Royal Gorge." I had almost surfeited myself with the mere prelude to the repast.   The best was brought on, when my appetite was, so to speak, appeased. But, what did appear, was too good to neglect, so I was soon at it again as before, and did not leave my perch until we had passed through all the glories which the Royal Gorge contained.

The climax was reached in a spot too narrow for a track by the side of the raging torrent.   Our railroad was suspended from the sides of the towering mountains by a huge iron construction, over which we passed, until wider space beyond, gave us again a hold on *terra firma.*

Through all this region there is also the evidence of energy and force of another kind.   One sees the deserted huts of the gold-hunters, who prospected, it may be in vain, or made their " pile and cleared out."

There is a terrible fascination in this eager hunt for wealth, and those who hunt all their lives, often get least, and die in misery.

I was once in Victor, the next town to Cripple Creek, and while there, heard, in the most casual way, that Tom Brennan, I think that was his name, had been found in the mountains, dead, by his own hand. His luck was gone, starvation stared him in the face, and, old, and hopeless, in his lone misery, he sought death, alone.

When one sees, away up on some apparently inaccessible height, an indication of fresh earth, and a black aperture at the top of it, and realizes that in that spot, some one, or it may be more, are digging and delving for a wealth that may never come, the thought is inevitable of possible ruined hopes, or of sudden wealth, as Fortune may frown or smile. But here, as well as everywhere, and in all relations of life, the poet's words come true,

"The many fail, the one succeeds."

It is well for us, however, that failures, which may be possible, never daunt us from effort, and the search, for that which the soul longs for. We picture to ourselves success ever. Failure, like death, too often comes, unannounced.

It is the spirit of daring and adventure which still peoples the lonely mines on the mountainsides; which fills the mining towns on their highest crests, and which keeps the miners busy, whether on their highest heights, or in the closeness of their deepest depths.

While on my way, a gentleman met me on the train, and pressed me to stop over at Leadville, promising that he would take me down the deepest gold mine in the place. I could not stay, even for that approach to the presence of all-powerful gold.

I am sure that the underground view of Leadville would be better than that which the sun looks upon. It is not an inviting-looking place. It lies on the great top surges of the mountains, having all the bleakness of a plain, and the rarefied atmosphere of the mountain summit, which it really is.

It is always a weird thing to look at the scenes of early mining days in Leadville, when the fame of the fabulous wealth therein, entered into men's brains, with an intoxication, like that of some Oriental drug. California Gulch looks like the dried bed of a mountain torrent. What must it have been when every inch of it was staked out in claims, and men, by men, close together, but widely separate in their interests, shovelled up the dirt, and peered with eager gaze therein for the yellow gold.

It is well to realize that even in Colorado, which is considered more a mining than an agricultural State, the farm products, at the present time, far

outweigh in value the entire annual output of the
mines.   The prosaic toil, as some may deem it,
of the spade, and the plough; and the pastoral
occupation of stock-raising and dairy farming, are
better wealth-makers than the pick of the miner,
or the labors of the mining engineer.

The great day of our run through the giant
attractions of the mountains comes to a close at
Pueblo, a busy railroad centre, where our track
bends to the north, and brings us at nightfall to
Colorado Springs.

When we remembered all the glories of the
day, the great mountain clefts through which we
passed, the roaring torrents which accompanied
us, the fantastic coloring of the rocks, and the
evidences of labor and energy which we had seen
on every hand; and remembered also the untold
wealth which lay concealed, whether gold and
silver, or rock oil, or the produce of ranch and
cattle range, our thoughts gathered up a splendid
impression of opulence, actual, and future.

Yet, wild and vast as it all was, we could not
help thinking also, that the nearest approach we
had anywhere seen, to the glories through which
we had passed, had been already presented to us
by the streets of New York.   Yes, it is like seeing
a Grand Cañon, to look from Murray Hill on

some October afternoon, down Fifth Avenue. There it all is,—the towering edifices at each side are the mountains, the crowd rushes on like the river,—all is color, life, and motion; and the blue haze of the autumn day gives vagueness and mystery to the descending perspective, as it comes to a point in Washington Square.

One sees the same effect also on lower Broadway, where the huge buildings, and the wealth and energy which they express, suggest ever to my mind the splendors of the great cañons of the West.

XX

WE found much to interest us in Colorado
Springs. It is a town of great fame as a health
resort, and lies on a splendid plateau, with the
background of the Rocky Mountains, and Pike's
Peak, in all its snowy splendor, in the middle distance.

Near by is Colorado City, and joining on to
that is Manitou, where lie the wonderful mineral springs, from which the city of " Colorado
Springs " gets its name.

The wise men who founded the city, knew well
that there was no room for expansion in the
Alpine clefts where the springs lie; and yet they
knew, too, their value as an attraction. Hence,
the shrewd wisdom to bravely adopt a *lucus
a non lucendo*, to call their town " Colorado

Springs." They had them not, it is true, but they were near at hand.

It is well that they thus decided for both site and name; for the place chosen, gives ample scope for wide streets, and all the room for expansion, which the coming years demand. As it is, the growth of the place has been phenomenal. It is hard to realize that the public buildings, the churches, the schools, and the splendid homes are all the result of a comparatively brief period.

After our vast journey, we were not in much of a mood for more aggressive sightseeing; but some of our party, bravely attempted the ascent of Pike's Peak, on the cog railway, just opened for the season.

When the party was near the summit, a furious snow-storm came down upon them. The track had been cleared of snow some days before, and huge piles of it lay on each side of the course, but this sudden storm gave fresh obstruction. Men were detailed to clear away the encumbrance, so as to get the train clear up to the adjacent summit; but as they were thus engaged in front, the snow-storm was rapidly filling in the track behind. It was fortunately observed that the dreadful possibility of being snowed up on that bleak height, was imminent; so all hands were called away from further effort to get farther on, and a speedy retreat was made to safety and a lower level, where snow was not. Our merry party had a good snow-balling time, while all this was going on, and did not know, until their return, the fearful possibilities from which they had escaped.

The view from Pike's Peak toward the east is magnificent. The memory of it will never leave me, as I saw it years ago. The vast plain of Kansas stretches out, more sublime even than the ocean. One can mark the winding water courses, by the trees which line their banks; and the dimness, which covers all the great distance, has a sublime effect.

As I descended in the cog train, a furious thunder-storm blotted all the landscape from the view; but soon the converging lines of the mountains became visible, the sun shone out once more from the west, and that great plain was spanned with a double rainbow, so huge, so brilliant, so all-embracing, that its like could not easily be seen, except under similar conditions, and those would be hard to match. It was the most splendid spectacle I have ever beheld.

We had two days at Colorado Springs and vicinity, and enjoyed to the full the charm of our

situation at Manitou, where our good car " Lucania " again found a pleasant anchorage.

The mineral springs at Manitou, are of iron and
soda. They are now all tamed and chained to
commerce; and the place, in the season (we were
too early for it), is a scene of excursions, and
merry-makings, and all that kind of life which delights in shows and curio shops, and restaurants
at all prices.

How sacred a place it must have been to the
wild children of the mountain and the plain, as
they sought its mystic retreat, for the sake of its
healing waters, and its strange, sparkling streams!
It was for them, indeed, from Manitou, the Great
Spirit.

From the parching drought of the burning summer sun, or the ice-bound cold of winter, they
could enter here, at any time, and find refreshment for their thirst, and healing for their wounds.

There surely must be a whole treasury of Indian
myth and legend clustering round this spot and
its wonderful sacred fountains, all well worth the
study of the antiquarian and the poet. I am confident that the place is as rich, in all such matters,
as ever Delphi was, or the sacred places of the
Greeks.

We were charmed, while at Manitou, by a visit

11

to a superb collection of minerals, beautifully arranged, and all, the product of Colorado. There is something especially attractive in mineral beauty. It took its form in the mystery of darkness, and there, in all its beauty, would remain forever, content to be. But man brings it to the light of day, and we are thrilled as we look at the perfect forms of the crystal, at the rich verdure of the velvet malachite, at the varied veinings of onyx and of agate, and at the many wonders which we admire, but cannot name.

We were told that this splendid collection had been purchased for ten thousand dollars, and was to be shown at the Paris Exhibition of 1900. It is well worthy of such a place.

While at Colorado Springs we had one or two splendid drives. We went through Glen Eyrie, the residence of General Palmer. The romantic place is kept generously open for carriages, but it is not permitted to any one to dismount, or drive in the roads marked private. It is a delightful spot, where nature is left yet in much of its wildness, and just enough of landscape gardening introduced to give a note of home and refinement. An eagle's nest, high up on the rocks, gives the name Glen Eyrie to the attractive place.

We also went to the Garden of the Gods. This is a great space hemmed in by huge crags, and covered all over with fantastic rock formations.

As we drove through, our coachman sounded out the names of the grotesque groups as we passed them by. It required but little imagination to improve on his list. Whatever the mind might fancy, the sandstone was ready to give. The rocks were as variable and changing as the clouds in " Hamlet." They might be whales, or bears, or dragons, or toadstools, or demons, or anything else vague and fantastic.

I can imagine how such a place would set a nervous person mad. Not, that it is not beautiful also, in a certain sense, but, the gibing, the mocking, the absurd prevails ; and one is almost shocked, even when in most sober mood. The mental distress, possible in such a place, seemed all concentrated in the face of a lone young bicyclist, with bicycle by his side, who eagerly questioned us as to the way to Manitou. He had lost his way amid these gruesome wonders, and although it was ludicrous to see his distress, one could not but sympathize with his misery, while lost in this wild, so full of monsters. I may here quote what Victor Hugo, in his " Alps and Pyrenees," says of sandstone. It would seem as if he was actually describing some of the fantastic forms which we saw in the Garden of the Gods.

" Sandstone," he says, " is the most interesting of stones. There is no appearance which it does not take, no caprice which it does not have, no dream which it does not realize. It has every shape; it makes every grimace. It seems to be animated by a multiple soul. Forgive me the expression with regard to such a thing.

" In the great drama of the landscape, sandstone plays a fantastic part. Sometimes it is grand and severe, sometimes buffoonlike; it bends like a wrestler, it rolls itself up like a clown; it may be a sponge, a pudding, a tent, a cottage, the stump of a tree; it has faces that laugh, eyes that look, jaws that seem to bite and munch the ferns; it seizes the brambles like a giant's fist suddenly issuing from the earth. Antiquity, which loved perfect allegories, ought to have made the statue of Proteus of sandstone.

" The aspects presented by sandstone, those curious copies of a thousand things which it makes, possess this peculiarity: the light of day does not dissipate them and cause them to vanish. Here at Pasajes, the mountain, cut and ground away by the rain, the sea, and the wind, is peopled by the sandstone with a host of stony inhabitants, mute, motionless, eternal, almost terrifying. Seated with outstretched arms on the summit of an inaccessible rock at the entrance of the bay, is a hooded hermit, who, according as the sky is clear or stormy, seems to be blessing the sea, or warning the mariners. On a desert plateau, close to heaven, among the clouds, are dwarfs, with beaks like birds, monsters with human shapes, but with two heads, of which one laughs and the other weeps—there where there is nothing to make one laugh and nothing to make one weep. There are the members of a giant, *disjecti membra gigantis;* here the knee, there the trunk and omoplate, and there, further off, the head. There is a big-paunched idol with the muzzle of an ox, necklets about its neck, and two pairs of short, fat arms, behind which some great bramble-bushes wave like fly-flaps. Crouching on the top of a high hill is a gigantic toad, marbled over by the lichens with yellow and livid spots, which opens a horrible mouth and seems to breathe tempest over the ocean.''

It was a regret to leave Colorado Springs, but dear home was before us, and Denver, which we reached in the darkness, brought us nearer there. .

XXI

Denver.—The Union Station.—The Departing Trains.—
The Beauty of Denver.—Dean Hart and the Cathedral.
—The Funeral Service.—Seeing Denver.

IT was quite late in the evening when we reached Denver; but late as it was, we could enjoy, for an hour or so, the handsome Union Station, and watch the trains, made up for their midnight start, east, west, north, and south. It is really a beautiful thing to see those various trains, awaiting their departure, side by side upon the tracks.

Their appointments are so splendid; the life exhibited so varied; and the lighted trains, the uniformed attendants, and the whole scene so interesting, that it is well worth observing. The quiet of the whole thing, too, is remarkable. It is all intensely busy, but almost noiseless and at rest. American force, ever quiet, is behind all. Off the trains go, as if by magic, just a little creeping, gentle motion at first; and then, the great steam monsters in front eat the ground, and in thunderous motion the long trains speed away, to their one, two, or even three thousand-mile destinations. How splendid it all is! To some, perhaps, a mere commonplace thing, but to me, ever a scene of deep interest, filled with human force, and freighted down with human cares, and hopes; with sorrows, too; and, let us hope, also, with many joys.

In the morning we could see how Denver looked by daylight. The little city is a beauty that need not fear the day. One gets such an agreeable impression of Denver from the very first. The great Union Station is attractive, and when one leaves it for home or hotel, one is greeted by a garden of living green, and by trees and shrubs in flourishing verdure. These gardens which greet one on emerging from the station, are like the beautiful initial letters one sees on old manuscripts, all glittering in gold and colors, inviting one to peruse and value the precious pages.

We had two lovely days in Denver, and our party scattered about at will. Some went to call on old friends, and cemented anew the ties which might rust, but could never break. Some went shopping, while others lounged in delicious idleness, without helm or oar, just drifting.

To visit Denver and not see Dean Hart at the Cathedral would be an irreparable loss. We called upon him, and found him, as he always is, genial, animated, and brimful of good humor and hospitality. Busy as he also always is, he yet found time to call at the " Lucania," and to tell more than one of his good stories.

Some of our party attended a missionary meeting of ladies, held in the Cathedral, and brought from thence impressions of earnest workers, of bright, telling speeches, and of much hospitable good cheer.

The Cathedral at Denver is a Romanesque structure, of quite stately proportions, with an effective interior; some very good stained glass; a choir screen of wrought iron, interesting in workmanship; and the whole place has a comfortable sumptuousness quite attractive. It is the intention to face the outside, some time or other, with native sandstone, and the interior also with some suitable material of more ornamental character.

I have a memory of a service held in that Cathedral, which in sad solemnity I have never seen surpassed.

It was the funeral of a gentleman who lost his life in the wild waters of the Grand Cañon of the Colorado. He was with a railroad surveying party; the boat he was in was upset, and the waters were so violent, that his body was instantly sucked down in the boiling depths, and never more was found.

His dear wife was in London, when the news reached her. At once she returned to Denver, and hoped that once more she would lay eyes on her beloved dead. But all in vain. No human hand could reach the depths, where all that was mortal of her love, was forever hidden.

In this sad condition of circumstances, it was determined to hold the funeral services, as if the body were present, to his wife and friends, as it was to God, Whose All-Seeing Eye beholds all depths.

The mourning group was met at the door of the church; the sentences were read as usual, proceeding up the aisle; the service went on in the accustomed manner, and the words of committal, "Earth to earth, ashes to ashes," were read, with the added awfulness of that body being we knew not where. The thrilling silence and tears of that congregation were almost painful as the words were uttered. Then came the final prayers, and, while we were yet on our knees, the organist, in deep, muffled tones, whispered out the Dead March in "Saul."

No one moved until all the strains of that sublime, yet simple wail of sorrow were ended; and
then, all rose in silence, and remained standing
until the mourning party had left the church.

It was such a funeral as few have ever seen
with all its strangeness, and its pathos. I have
never forgotten it.

Perhaps during our stay in Denver, our trip on
the street-cars gave us most pleasure, and this,
too, at little cost. On a sign at the Brown Palace
Hotel we saw an inscription—"Seeing Denver,
Twenty-Five Miles, Twenty-Five Cents." There
was genius in that simple, fetching announcement.
At the hour named for starting we got on board
an electric car, and away we went. We were
switched in all directions through the business
part of Denver, by all the public buildings, round
and round, and then away out to the suburbs.
At one point we had a magnificent view of the
mountains, with Pike's Peak, eighty miles away,
snow-crowned, and plainly visible.

We had a magnificent ride, and it seemed even
more than twenty-five miles. During it all we
were accompanied by the proprietor of the enterprise, a keen-looking young fellow, who acted as
guide, giving us his information, in a sort of lan-
guid manner, which made his witty sallies more

witty still. His closing. speech, in which he intimated that his sole and only motive for getting
up this really convenient system of " seeing Denver " was for our special benefit, was irresistibly
comic in its assumed seriousness. He deserved
all he got from the trip, and we wished him the
extensive patronage he deserves.

When we left Denver it was as if all the special
novelties of the trip had come to an end, and the
sooner home the better; such is the effect of
satiety even in the luxurious travel we had been
enjoying.

We left Denver, teeming as it is with interest,
the Paris of the West; and night settled down
upon us as we bore directly east from Pueblo.

XXII

Through Kansas.—Kansas City.—The Cattle Yards.—The
    Bluffs.—The Fight between the Merrimac and the
    Monitor.

OUR homeward route took us through the
southern part of Kansas. It was refreshing to
see the vast, verdant plains which greeted us in
the early morning light. It is a great and glorious land, and all day long we watched the farms,
the houses, the villages, and the towns, as we
journeyed onward, ever onward. The whole country was in richest green, resulting from the recent
almost too profuse rains. But nothing in Kansas
goes by halves. It is a drought or a deluge, a
dead calm or a cyclone. How can it be otherwise! From the Rockies to the Alleghanies, it is
all a vast, curving plain. The fluid air, in such
a wide area, when influenced in any way, must be
on a gigantic scale. A tilt of half an inch at one
point, will be a mile in height, thousands of miles
farther on. Such a proportion of oscillation tells.

One could but dream of coming empire and
Western enterprise and power yet unthought of,
while lounging about in our flying train, homeward, still homeward, every moment, over those
vast plains. We had ample leisure for this delicious, idle dreaming. We looked on, as if we
were denizens of another world, as we saw the
bustle at passing stations, and the play of varied
human interests which disported themselves before our magnificent heedlessness of it all. We
were cut off, for the nonce, from all such care
or thought, flying onward, filled with pleasure,
to our Eastern home.

It was night when we made our first stop of any
length. That was at Kansas City. We here
crossed the " Big Muddy," or the Missouri
River, swollen by the extraordinary rains, and
looking more than ever like a tawny lion.

As we neared Kansas City we could see across
the waters of the river to the other side, where
myriads of cattle wandered like spectres, awaiting
further immediate shipment east, or, the nearer
end of the adjacent slaughter-houses. How sad
it all seemed. The cattle, magnified by the inter-
vening air, loomed up hugely across the brown
waters of the river. They seemed like victims of
destiny, conscious of their doom; and the sullen

river, and the shades of ·the falling day, gave fitting color and setting to the melancholy picture.

I asked a lady by my side, " Do you see all those cattle ? " " Yes," said she; " I cannot bear to look at them."   Our thoughts were the same.

How fortunate it is for us that our poor, four-footed brethren cannot probe our motives as we fatten our flocks and herds, and tend them with tireless assiduity! The beasts do love us, perhaps, and think us good and kind, and their best friend. I wonder, as they face the knife or the mallet, at the sublime moment of the end, are they awakened at last to the true inwardness of their false friend, man!

All this great prairie journey was a pleasant contrast to the great deserts and mountains we had passed, since we flew down through Jersey, the Southern States, across Texas and Arizona, out to California and the Rockies with all their wonders.

Our stay in Kansas City was limited to a few hours, but in that time some of us ventured out on the streets, which were not very inviting, down on the bottom lands among the grime of the railroad tracks.

Kansas City lies, the best part of it, on high bluffs overlooking the great Missouri River, and its tributary, at this point, the Kaw. It is really a picturesque place, and capable of being beautified to any extent. The bluffs are quite precipitous, and on their shelving sides a number of squatters have settled, with their nondescript cabins and huts, giving a sort of rag-fair look to the general aspect of the town as seen as a whole. But the City Fathers have awakened to the fact, that those precipitous bluffs can be made highly ornamental, by green sod and trees and flowers. A great park plan has been projected for all those curving spaces, and ere long the city will be made unique and beautiful by those winding, aspiring, and splendid plantations, out of which the homes, the churches, and public buildings will rise as from a garden.

In our brief stay we called on our dear and old-time friend, the Rev. J. Stewart Smith, of St. Mary's, or, rather, I should say he called on us, for, having announced our coming by telegraph, he was there at the station to meet us.

It so happened that a day or two before he had written, for one of the local papers, his recollection of the great fight between the Merrimac and the Monitor in Hampton Roads in the year 1862.

How much has transpired since then!

In view of it all, and our Cuban War, still on,

all now happily over as I write, I thought that my dear friend's recollections would be of interest, as that of an eye-witness of that great first battle between armored ships.

Here is what he says:

"One of my earliest recollections is of the United States frigate, Merrimac, which anchored off Norfolk in 1855 before making her first voyage. Like most small boys, I was deeply interested in anything that would float, and when one of the officers took me on board and showed me everything to be seen, explaining, so far as was possible to make a child understand, the workings of a warship, I was perfectly happy. I asked many questions, and ever afterward I felt a peculiar interest—almost a sense of ownership—in that vessel.

"At the beginning of the war the Merrimac was again in Hampton Roads, undergoing repairs at the navy yard, just across the river from Norfolk. One Saturday night early in April, 1861, Norfolk was abandoned by the Federal forces. The next day the dry dock was blown up, the navy yard, all the smaller crafts, the Pennsylvania, perhaps the largest vessel in the service—too large, in fact, to be seaworthy, but which had been for years used as a training-ship at the port—and the Merrimac were set on fire.

"I can never forget the scene on that Sunday

morning. Words cannot describe the excitement
of the people. The harbor was dotted with burning vessels; the ear was startled by repeated ex-
plosions, and the whole scene was backed by a
mass of roaring flame devouring shops, store-
houses, and sheds about the navy yard.

" The fires were brightly burning when, with
hundreds, I found myself on the ground, which
was still hot, picking out nails from the touch-
holes of the heavy guns hastily abandoned. Some
were properly spiked, nails had been simply
dropped into others, and many had not received
even this attention. But the thing that interested me more than all else was the flames still
licking the black sides of the huge Pennsylvania,
and the graceful form of ' my ship,' the Merrimac,
now burning to the water's edge.

" The Confederate Government was quick to
take advantage of the situation. The navy yard
was rebuilt, and the dry dock repaired. The plan
of rebuilding the Merrimac was proposed, but was
found impracticable on account of the expense,
although her hull was almost uninjured. Lieu-
tenant John Mercer Brooks and Joseph L. Porter
then presented a plan for converting her into a
floating battery, which was accepted. A high
fence was built around the dock and the work
began. Great secrecy was maintained, but I was
able to gain admission two or three times, and to
look with wondering eyes on the strange struc-

ture.   The hull was cut down to the water-line, a
low deck was built out at the bow and stern,
heavy oak timbers were set up like the rafters of
a house inclined at an angle of about 45 degrees,
and these were covered with several thicknesses
of railroad iron, which extended into the water.
When finished, the vessel looked like a long, black
roof with the top cut off so as to be flat.   Around
this ran a light iron rail, a wide funnel rose about
the middle, and a low pyramidal structure pierced
with small sight-holes served to protect the pilot.
As I recall her, she carried two guns forward and
three aft on each side, and one or two at both
bow and stern.   She had no mast, except a short
one at the stern for the flag.   The bow was
pointed without curving, and an oak ram, pro-
tected by a heavy iron shoe, extended forward
under water.   Her name was changed to the Vir-
ginia, but every one spoke of her still as the Merrimac.   One day it was announced that she was
ready to go out, and the next that she was a failure.   For weeks reports of the most conflicting
character were in circulation, and no one could
find out anything definite.

" The report of her failure had, however, generally been credited, when on Saturday morning,
March 8, 1862, the news came that she was going
out.   It spread like wildfire, and soon every one
in the city was wrought up to the highest pitch
of excitement.   Slowly she steamed down the

river, looking like a floating shed, and with her went the Jamestown, the Patrick Henry, and several other vessels that made up the Confederate fleet.   The town was wild; whistles blew, bells rang, guns were fired, people shouted, the air was full of flags and hats and cries.   Every one who could do so hastened toward Sewell's Point to see the expected battle.   Vehicles of every description were pressed into service, and those who could not ride set out to walk through the sand.

" The Congress and the Cumberland rode at anchor a few hundred yards from shore, and not far away the Minnesota and the Roanoke.   These vessels were a part of the United States blockading fleet.   As the Merrimac drew near, we on the shore could see the preparations making on the wooden ships to receive their strange foe. The guns of the Congress roared out, and those of the Cumberland joined in the chorus, but although fired at short range, their shot fell harmless from the iron sides of the Merrimac.   The flash of cannon, and the exploding shells, were clearly seen when the smoke would lift.

" As if in disdain of the puny weapons turned against her, the ironclad went slowly on till she seemed to bury herself in the side of the Cumberland.   She had rammed the big ship.   The guns roared again and again, but without effect, and lurching forward, the Cumberland sank in fifty

feet of water, her masthead, from which floated the
flag, remaining visible above the waves.

"The Merrimac then turned her attack upon
the Congress, and the other Confederate ships
began to engage in the battle. The Congress
soon ran aground and was practically helpless
against the tremendous fire that was turned against
her. About four o'clock her flag was hauled
down, and she was boarded by a Confederate
officer. Later she was discovered to be on fire in
several places, and, her magazine exploding, she
was destroyed. The Minnesota was next assailed.
She also ran aground, and the Merrimac could not
reach her, but the wooden fleet poured in shot and
shell, inflicting serious damage. As night was now
drawing on, the Confederate fleet withdrew, having
carried everything before it.

"Early Sunday morning the Merrimac again
turned seaward, evidently intending to attack the
Minnesota. I hurried down to a point on the
south side of the bay, from which I could get an
unobstructed view of whatever might take place.
The Monitor had arrived the night before. I
had never seen the strange-looking craft, but the
minute I laid eyes on it I knew what it was.
Young as I was, I realized that I was about to
witness the most remarkable naval battle that was
ever fought up to that time—the first encounter
between ironclads.

"The Merrimac was the pride of my heart.

When I saw the Monitor I wondered what the result of the fight would be. With a glass in my hand I shivered with excitement as they approached each other. The two strangest vessels on the sea were face to face. A cheese-box on a plank, all painted black, not inaccurately describes the Monitor's appearance. She was much smaller and more active than the Confederate vessel, and carried only two guns, but these could be pointed in any direction by the revolving of her turret. Quickly they engaged, and the fight soon became furious.

" The guns on the Merrimac poured forth broadside after broadside. The shot and shells glanced off the turret of the Monitor and fell harmless into the water. In the same way, the heaviest shot from the Monitor's guns bounded off the slanting sides of the Merrimac, like foul balls from a player's bat. Sometimes it looked as if they were in actual contact. Even then the shells did no harm of any consequence to either vessel.

" The Minnesota joined in the conflict, and fired her broadside of fifty guns into the Merrimac. It seemed to me that every shot struck, but they all fell harmless from the invulnerable sides of the ironclad. The battle was waged with terrific rapidity of action. Now the two craft seemed joined together, now the Monitor would run around the Merrimac, as if trying to find a weak spot. The sound of the cannonading was deafening, even at my distance.

" The Merrimac presently withdrew. The crowd on the shore trembled and asked what the matter could be. Was she defeated ? There was only a moment's suspense, but it seemed like an hour. The answer came soon. Suddenly swinging around, the Merrimac paused for a minute, then steamed with full head against the Monitor. The little ' cheese-box ' staggered from the blow, but soon righted and continued firing, practically unharmed. When the Cumberland was rammed, the iron shoe that covered the Merrimac's ram was torn off, and so she had nothing but the oak foundation to oppose to the iron sides of the Monitor.

" This was about the last incident of the fight. Shortly afterward the two vessels drew apart, the smoke lifted, and neither of them showed any disposition to renew the battle. The Monitor headed toward Fortress Monroe, and the Merrimac steamed toward the Minneapolis, as if to continue the fight, but passed on without attacking her, and rested under the guns of the Confederate battery at Craney Island.

" Norfolk was evacuated by the Confederates two months later, the navy yard was burned, and many ships were destroyed. An effort was made to get the Merrimac to Richmond, but it was impossible to take her over the bar at the entrance

of the James River.   Just at daylight, Sunday
morning, May 11th, we in Norfolk were awakened
by an explosion whose meaning all quickly
guessed.   The Merrimac had been blown up by
her commander, Josiah Tattnall, and so effectively
destroyed that no fragments sufficient to reveal
the details of her construction were ever recov-
ered.

" The Monitor was lost in a storm off Cape
Hatteras at midnight of December 31 of the same
year (1862).   The two ironclads, which in a single
day had changed the face of war and revolution-
ized the navies of the world, thus found early
graves."

XXIII

WE reached St. Louis in the early morning hour, after a pleasant night's rest on our good car "Lucania." The country approaching St. Louis looks rich and luxuriant, with fine trees, and well-established country places. The effect of an older culture was at once apparent, as we approached this great city of the West.

Our car anchorage was in the magnificent Union Station, a very large place, indeed, and excellently managed. Some of our party again took to the street cars, and in that democratic fashion, saw much of the town.

At a later period in the day, some of us had a lovely carriage ride through the best residential portion of the city.

We were more than surprised at the beautiful

streets, lined with spacious palaces, each in its own separate grounds. To a New Yorker's eyes, this roominess of arrangement, was especially attractive. Charming effects were produced by beautiful gardens in the middle of certain secluded streets, with fountains and flowers, all kept in beautiful order. The private grounds around the separate houses were in like good shape. All looked sumptuous, and in the best possible taste.

To drive into one of these " Places " through the ornamental gates, and see the richness of the central parterre, the well-kept streets at each side, and the generous sidewalks and rich verdure surrounding the houses, was a new sensation. The general verdict was, that even in New York, there was nothing like that.

All this urban development is the work of the last fifteen or twenty years. Such communal and united display was not the custom of the early French settlers. They loved the enclosed privacy of their own grounds, as in New Orleans, but times have changed, and the dwellers in St. Louis have changed with them.

We drove also in Forest Park, a really beautiful place, with a spaciousness truly magnificent.

Our stay in St. Louis was barely a day. We took a glimpse at the river front, once a busy

scene with its fleet of steamboats running from
the northwestern wilds, by way of the Missouri
and its tributaries, and down to the Gulf of
Mexico, by way of the Mississippi.   But the
glory of the steamboating days is gone forever.
The iron horse now does the greater part of the
carrying trade, and great railroad bridges span the
Father of Waters at several points, and more are
coming.

I took a little independent trip from St. Louis
by rail, to Alton, on the Illinois side.   It just
took three hours; one to get there, one there, and
one to return.

It was many long years since I resided in Alton,
and it was with a sort of fearfulness that I made
the excursion.   Would any one remember me ?
Were my friends yet living ?   And so on.   I
crossed the great railroad bridge over the Mississippi, and up on the east bank to Alton, which
lies just above the confluence of the two great
rivers.   I passed through, on the Illinois side,
what seemed a continuous series of manufacturing
settlements, all emphasizing the vast development
of industrial enterprises in the West.

On arriving at Alton, the changed aspect of all
was most apparent.   The river front—where in
old times I had seen the steamboats line up, and

watched their loading and unloading, picturesque by day or by night, but especially attractive when seen under the glare of torches, and enlivened by the songs of the negro hands—was now, almost, unused. The railroad tracks dominated everything, down to the water's edge.

I wandered off at random through the streets, until I came to the old familiar Alton Bank, which looked exactly the same. I entered to inquire after friends, and as the clerk was obligingly giving me information, I asked him if he knew a former clerk, Mr. W——, who was there years before. "Oh, yes," said he; "he is now our president." By this time a pleasant face looked fixedly at me, and, in a moment, an outstretched hand grasped mine, and my old friend was calling me by name, and we were once more young men again, when, in the old time, music was our bond of fellowship, and all that that involves.

While we were speaking—the bank president and myself—a lady, with her little girl, entered the office, and again my name was called. "I have been following you in the street," she said. "I knew it must be you, but I could scarcely believe my eyes." It was the daughter of a dear friend of years long gone, and her daughter was by her side.

How lovely it all seemed to be thus recognized, and to bind together afresh the ties of years that had fled!

But my hour in Alton was almost up. I could only look at the outside of the dear old church where I once worshipped. My friend of the bank brought me, to the train, as a little gift of remembrance, a book called " Poems of the Piasa," by Frank C. Riehl. It contained also a number of other kindred poems of Western life.

The Piasa was a dreadful, winged monster, which inhabited the banks of the Mississippi at Alton in ages past. A note in the volume I received might here be quoted. It is as follows:

" The region along the shores on both sides of the Mississippi, between the points of the confluence of the Illinois and Missouri rivers with the Father of Waters, is particularly rich in legendary stories concerning the life and habits of the powerful tribes of Indians who were the original owners of these fertile valley lands. Along the bluffs on the Illinois side are numberless burial places where the bones of thousands of ' the first Americans ' repose, while the valleys and prairie-stretches for some distance back from the river, afford constant reminders of their presence and handiwork in the dim ages of the past.

" From the time of the earliest frontier expeditions, this locality has been conspicuous among the chronicles for the number and peculiar charm of the folk-lore stories handed down from one generation to another, and held in almost sacred reverence by the Indians. And, among these, dating from the famous expedition of Marquette, none is more striking and interesting than that of the Piasa Bird. That this was more than a mere myth is attested by the evidence of many early settlers, who got the story in minute detail from the Indians themselves; and by the painting that remained upon the face of the perpendicular bluffs within the present limits of the city of Alton, until quarried away just about the close of the first half of this century."

The Indian legend referred to is of a fearful, winged monster, who swooped down upon his prey, making his aery on the great cliffs at Alton. The tribes were in deadly terror of this great creature, whose fearful power seized their bravest warriors, as well as their most beautiful maidens, in his deadly talons. At last, a chief, named Ouatoga, conceived the bold design to place himself in the way of the monster, a sacrifice for the safety of his race; while twelve of the best archers, should lie concealed near by, and slay the monster with their united arrows, as he rose in air with his prey. This, the legend says, was done, and a rude picture of the monster might be seen on the bluffs at Alton until recent times.

I cannot help thinking, however, that the story is, after all, a myth of the dreaded tornado so frequent in the West. I have a photograph of such a storm, taken in Iowa, and the huge, involving clouds, spread out like wings, and, the descending funnel or waterspout, reaching to the earth, destroying all it touches, exactly resembles a huge monster bird, in awful and sudden flight, devouring everything before it. The discharge of the arrows at the monster, thus killing it, may be a hint of the well-known fact, that any sudden impact upon a whirlwind, in its funnel-shaped motion, will destroy its vibrations and hence its progress. A rifle-shot, sent into a whirling dust pillar on the great plains, will reduce the dreadful thing at once to a clatter of falling dust and pebbles, and a dead heap of harmless stuff. So much for a theory anyway.

I returned to St. Louis by the Missouri side, having with me my lady friend and her little daughter. The route took us over the great bridges which span the two rivers just above their confluence. It was grand in its effect, to pass over two such great streams coming close together from their distant sources, soon to mingle in one mighty torrent, emptying itself more than a thousand miles away, into the Gulf of Mexico.

It was all a sort of enchanted excursion, waking up many memories of a past, so far removed from the present hour.

Our train brought us into the great Union Station, from which I had set out three hours before.

While in this splendid station I had the good fortune to have a long chat with the superintendent thereof. He tried to tell me, I should say, he did tell me, of its wonderful construction, its great extent, its complex machinery, its electrical appliances, its vast detail of business. I have only an impression of the sweet gentleness which so patiently explained all to me, and of the myriad ramifications which I could see, could but dimly understand, and vaguely remember. He has my thanks and grateful memory for his kindness.

We also saw in the St. Louis depot a thoroughly interesting American affair. It was an educational car, run by two or three bright young fellows, who quite captivated us by their intelligence and spirit. They were occupying a beautiful private car, fitted up as an office and a dwelling; and were travelling over the country in the interest of a great institution called " The International Correspondence Schools." It opened up before one a marvellous vista of business energy and splendid results. A circular, which we brought away with us, stated that instruction was given by this method in 42 courses, to some 40,000 students in 137 States and countries. The inside of the circular contained ten headings, and each heading had four lines of detailed information, looking like quatrains of poetry. I take at random one of them, as a sample, under the heading

SUPERIORITY

Students can be taught wherever the mails can go.
Each student regulates his own hours of study.
Written lessons qualify for written examinations.
The method cultivates memory, brevity, accuracy and independence.

It really did seem all like poetry, full of resplendent possibilities, to see the specimen books produced by the students; and, above all, it was poetical to see those young men in charge, so very young and yet so full of confidence, so intelligent, and so keen. They were at once at their ease with our party, and ere we left St. Louis, at ten o'clock at night, they visited us, and with mandolin music, and college songs, we wiled away a pleasant hour.

At ten o'clock we departed from St. Louis, passing through the tunnel, and out on the great bridge, from whence we looked at the mighty flood of the Father of Waters, far beneath us, reflecting in its turbid depths the lights of St. Louis, which were soon hidden from our sight, as we rolled out into the darkness, over the prairies of Illinois.

13

XXIV

IT was well on in Sunday morning when we
reached our next stopping-place, Columbus, Ohio,
where we stayed until Monday forenoon.

The morning light, as we journeyed on in the
early hours, showed us the smiling country in its
Sabbath rest. It was all such a contrast to the
far West, and the Pacific Slope, and not an un-
grateful one.

We were passing through Ohio, which, one
might say, is no longer the West, but the centre of
our land. It is a glorious country, rich, fertile,
and prosperous-looking.

Columbus quite pleased us, by the evidences of
its bustling activities and improvements; as well
as by a certain old-fashioned dignity and state.
It is the governmental seat of Ohio, and has some

quite respectable public buildings, all done in the
American-Greek-Classic style—rows of pillars,
pediments, and all that—which, I confess, I like
better than the strained effort after effect, seen in
some more modern structures.

A new piece of architecture at Columbus, however, the beautiful railroad station, was charming.
It is full of beauty, like a rich Italian palace, all
warm with golden carvings, yellow marble walls,
and mosaic pavements.

The interior effect of the waiting-rooms was exquisite, with the arched and coffered roof, and the
graceful outlines of all.

On Sunday night we all attended church, where
we heard a good sermon, and joined, with keen
relish, in a fine choral service, rendered by a well-
trained surpliced choir of men and boys. The
leader of the choir evidently had a heart for the
noble effects of Gregorian music, while not such a
purist as to rule out all modern compositions. In
this he was right. Gregorian music is like salt,
really necessary as a healthful adjunct in church
song, but too much of it is as bad as none at all.

It was toward evening when we reached Pitts-
burg, where we made but a short stay; and in
the early morning hour we were once more at the
Pennsylvania Depot in Jersey City, where we took

reluctant leave of each other and our good car
" Lucania."

Sleep had refreshed us, as we flew, all uncon-
scious, through the splendid scenery of the Alleghanies. But what were such mountains to us
now, who had seen the Rockies; and what was
the Horseshoe Curve, compared to the daring engineering of Colorado railroads! Nothing. We
were more than satisfied with all we had seen.

But before closing this scattering record of our
" Flight in Spring," surely it will be well to look
back, once more, at its pleasant hours, and sweet
companionship.

In those six weeks of our trip, equal almost to
a lifetime of contact, under ordinary circumstances, how well we got to know each other.
Surely the more each knew of each, the more did
trifling fault fade away, and clear goodness come
out into pleasing prominence. Was it not so ?

So that when we came to part at the station, it
was with a regret for that parting, and a hope
that friendships were cemented on our journey,
which nothing ever could dissever.

Let us think, too, with gratitude of the un-
wearying attention given to our comfort by Mr.
Payson, in whose charge were all the details of
our transportation, involving so much of most

serious importance, as well for our safety, as our comfort. How wonderful to think that our eight thousand miles of travel was all conducted like clockwork, with entire reliability, and precision, from point to point, across the continent and back again, without hitch or accident.

Then we must remember the Pullman employees, to whom the whole journey was but an episode, in lives of such journeys; and yet how enthusiastic and attentive they were, at all times.

And we must remember Delia and Charles, in their sphere of usefulness, ever ready and willing to carry out the hospitable intentions of our good host and hostess.

It is all over, our " Flight in Spring," with all its pleasant incidents. Some of the sweetest moments were, when we turned in upon ourselves for amusement and pleasure, at the evening hours, when formal sightseeing was over; or in those hours of travel, when the eyes refused to gaze longer on the flying landscape.

Then came the Nonsense Verses, and the Stories, and the Songs, and the Machine Poetry, and all the fun. Shall we not gather up some of those trifles, as worthy of preservation in our record? Yes, certainly we will.

We will first start out with the machine poetry.

Rhymes were furnished, which were these dreadful collocations, "give, live, dove, love, merry, cherry, go, slow, tease, squeeze, muddle, fuddle." A hopeless list surely.

Dear Fred, who said he could not write poetry, evolved the following:

POEM BY FRED

And when a pretty orange he did give,
He thought it was too sweet to live,
So he gave it to his dove
To ever sustain their love.

One day when all was merry,
He gave to her a cherry ;
And he said she should not go,
For fear it would be slow.

First he began to tease,
Then he began to squeeze,
Until there was a muddle—
Soon afterwards a fuddle.

This realistic effort was received with rounds of applause.   The next poetic effort on the procrustean rhymes was by Miss Hayden, as follows:

POEM BY MISS HAYDEN

Oh, why should I give,
Or expect me to live,
When you called me a dove,
Yet you now cease to love ?

I once was so merry,
My lips like a cherry,
I wept when you'd go,
And my heart beat so slow.

Then at once you would tease,
And kiss me, and squeeze,—
But—my brain's in a muddle,
And—you in a fuddle.

This effort, too, was greeted with approbation, and its tenderness duly appreciated.

But the Nonsense Verses were the best fun. One would shout out a line, an additional line would come from some one else, and by the time the whole thing was complete, it would be hard to discriminate as to who was the author.

Here is one hurled at me:

There was a Canon named Knowles,
Whose mission it was to save souls ;
        When out on this trip,
        He said, " Let them rip,
We'll save them all yet from the coals."

Some of our young ladies were deeply interested in the sailor boys at war, and for their benefit this nonsense had wing:

There was a young lady named Harding,
Whose sweetheart, the nation was guarding.
        The rumor of war,
        Went to her heart's core
For fear he'd be lost while bombarding.

These verses, too, have a maritime flavor:

> There was a young lady of nerve,
> Who bet on the Naval Reserve.
>   She got a flat cap
>   Like that of her chap,
> And said, "This our love will preserve."

We had lots of others, and ever so many good stories, but it is time to end. This last must suffice for the Nonsense Verses:

> There was a young lady *en route*,
> Who wanted to go on a toot,
>   So she jumped off the ca—ah
>   When no one was ne—ah,
> And feasted on candy and fruit.

This was the favorite refrain of all, for its reckless suggestions, and the special intonations of its third and fourth lines. Its echoes would sound out in the most unexpected connections—

> "So she jumped off the ca—ah
> When no one was ne—ah,"

and then would come a merry peal of laughter.

Sometimes the laughter even, would cease, and, we were all so free and unaffected, that siestas were taken, quite unceremoniously, when silence would settle down upon our party.

In such a quiet interval, one of our fair sleepers inspired the following lines, as she lay at rest, on the couch in the dining-room. This is what the poet said:

TO ETHEL ASLEEP

Our car glides on with giddy speed,
  But Ethel feels no motion;
Her soul and body take no heed,
  Wrapt still, in sleep's deep ocean.

And as I gaze on her sweet face,
  So placid, true and tender;
The wish for her I fain would trace
  Is this—May Heaven defend her!

'Mid all the whirling cares of life,
  May peaceful rest come to her;
And sleep, no matter what the strife,
  Be ever near to woo her.

With some such wish as this for all of us, I would like to close the record of this " Flight in Spring."

When spring, and summer, and autumn, and winter, will for us have forever fled away, then may we all find comfort, after life's wanderings are over, in this restful thought, as our great journey shall end:

"He giveth His beloved sleep."

But other thoughts also come to me, as I recall the splendid advantages of such a trip as our " Flight in Spring." It was a revelation, to pass from ocean to ocean, over our own broad land. It filled one's soul with enthusiasm, as one thought of the opportunities, the responsibilities, the duties, and the prospects of our citizenship.

It made me long that such " Flights in Spring," or in any season, might be more widely enjoyed, so that many more might realize the immense splendor and power of our great land.

For such purposes I would wish that there were instituted " Pilgrimages of Patriotism," which would bring representative men, from ocean to ocean, from seashore to centre, and from centre to seashore, at stated and solemn periods; thus emphasizing the sense of national citizenship, and the splendid and indissoluble union of our States.

I have read that among the Zuñi Indians it was a sacred law that some of their tribe should, each year, pour the waters of the Pacific into those of the Atlantic. The task was accomplished, despite of all difficulties, arising from tribal contests, or opposing forces. It was a symbol of union, touching as it was simple, and might again be revived among us, to emphasize the glorious bond of citizenship in this our land; a bond, which we felt continually, through our eight thousand miles of travel, in our " Flight in Spring."

ITINERARY

Lv.	New York......Wed. Apr.	13....	9.30 A.M.
Arr.	Thomasville. ..Thu. "	14....	2.35 P.M.
Lv.	" ....Sat. "	16....	2.45 "
Arr.	New Orleans....Sun. "	17....	9.20 "
Lv.	" " ....Mon. "	18....	8.40 "
Arr.	San Antonio ....Tue. "	19....	5.30 "
Lv.	" " ....Wed. "	20....	5.15 "
Arr.	El Paso........Thu. "	21....	3.45 "
Lv.	" " ....Fri. "	22....	2.35 "
Arr.	Los Angeles ....Sat. "	23....	9.20 "
Lv.	" " ....Tue. "	26....	2.00 "
Arr.	San Diego ...... " "	"	6.20 "
Lv.	" " .....Thu. "	28....	7.00 A.M.
Arr.	Los Angeles .... " "	" ....11.15 "
Lv.	" " .... " "	" .... 4.00 P.M.
Arr.	Santa Barbara .. " "	" .... 8.30 "
Lv.	" " ..Sat. "	30....	8.15 A.M.
Arr.	Brentwood......Sun. May	1....	9.00 "
Lv.	" ....Mon. "	2....	9.47 "
Arr.	San Francisco... " "	" ....12.15 P.M.
Lv.	" " ...Fri. "	6....10.40 A.M.
Arr.	Palo Alto....... " "	" ....11.59 "
Lv.	" " .... " "	" .... 4.44 P.M.
Arr.	San José .... .. " "	" .... 5.20 "
Lv.	" " ....Mon. "	9....11.00 A.M.

Arr. Santa Cruz	Mon.	May 9....	1.45 P.M.
Lv. " "	"	" "....	4.35 "
Arr. Del Monte......	"	" "....	6.30 "
Lv. " "	Wed.	" 11....	6.51 "
Arr. San José	"	" "....	9.07 A.M.
Lv. " "	"	" "....	1.15 P.M.
Arr. Oakland Pier...	"	" "....	3.45 "
Lv. " " ...	Thu.	" 12....	8.37 A.M.
Arr. Ogden	Fri.	" 13....	5.00 P.M.
Lv. "	"	" "....	6.20 "
Arr. Salt Lake City ..	"	" "....	7.30 "
Lv. " " " .	Sat.	" 14....	7.40 "
Arr. Colorado Sp'gs .	Sun.	" 15....	6.46 "
Lv. " " .	Mon.	" 16....	5.00 "
Arr. Manitou	"	" "....	6.45 "
Lv. "	Tue.	" 17....	7.07 "
Arr. Denver	"	" "....	9.15 "
Lv. "	Thu.	" 19....	7.00 "
Arr. Kansas City....	Fri.	" 20....	6.00 "
Lv. " " ...	"	" "....	9.00 "
Arr. St. Louis.......	Sat.	" 21....	7.10 A.M.
Lv. " "	"	" "....	10.00 P.M.
Arr. Columbus	Sun.	" 22....	11.20 A.M.
Lv. "	Mon.	" 23....	11.35 "
Arr. New York	Tue.	" 24....	7.43 "

www.ingramcontent.com/pod-product-compliance
Lightning Source LLC
Chambersburg PA
CBHW031954060726
47497CB00016B/2093